Abstract Casualty

Shandra Higheagle Mystery
Book 14

Paty Jager

Windtree Press
Hillsboro, Oregon

Copyright

This is a work of fiction, Names, characters, places, and incidents either are the product of the author's imagination or are used fictitiously, and any resemblance to actual persons living or dead, business establishments, events, or locales, is entirely coincidental.

ABSTRACT CASUALTY

Contact Information: info@windtreepress.com

Windtree Press
Hillsboro, Oregon
http://windtreepress.com

Cover Art by Christina Keerins

Published in the United States of America

ISBN   978-1-950387-90-8

Also available in ebook.

Special Thanks to:

Judy Melinek, M.D.

Crime Scene Writers Yahoo Group

And my husband for finally going to Hawaii with me.

Chapter One

The expectant faces on the crowd of artists gathered in the makeshift art gallery at a mall in Līhuʻe, Kauaʻi, Hawaii, had Shandra Higheagle Greer's stomach churning. She'd rather be on the receiving side of the juror's thoughts than be the juror.

She'd bumped into a college classmate at an art show in California eight months ago. Leilani Brown had suggested Shandra be the judge for the Kauaʻi Art Society's annual juried show. They paid for her flight, and her friend, Leilani, was housing she and Ryan for the week-and-a-half that it took to judge the entries, make decisions, and be at the grand opening this Saturday.

Talking about the pieces that she'd passed to be in the exhibition had been easy. They all had unique techniques that showed passion and all things that good art should have. It was talking about the pieces that didn't make it that had her stalling.

Especially, one piece.

She'd met Patrick James the day he'd brought his abstract painting in to be dropped off. He'd told her about the story of the painting, but she hadn't been able to see what he'd conveyed in words. She'd found the piece flat and void of emotion or sense of anything. How did she convey this without hurting the man's ego and perhaps keeping him from working on his chosen art form?

"There is one piece left for you to tell us your thoughts," Brendan Darnell, the president of the art society board, said, holding up Patrick's large, garish painting in primary colors.

Ryan stood at the back of the room. He'd told her she'd do a great job as a juror. Shandra shot a glance toward her husband who knew she'd dreaded this moment. He gave her a thumbs up.

"I feel this work could have used a bit more movement and emotion. If you study the pieces I chose, you'll see there is a fluidity and life to them. This piece is titled, 'A Child's World', yet, other than the bold primary colors, which I liked, it showed nothing of the vitality of a child, or emotion." She glanced at Patrick.

The man's face had become as red as the lackluster swipe of crimson paint on the canvas.

She hastily added, "Keep painting with honesty and passion."

The man grabbed his painting and shoved through the crowd, stopping in front of Leilani. "This is your fault! You asked your friend here to make sure I didn't get in the show!" He poked a finger at the woman.

Ryan stepped over to the confrontation. "You can either apologize or leave."

Patrick glared at Ryan before he jabbed his finger

around the room in several directions. "You'll all be sorry I'm not in this show." He strode to the glass doors, shoved them open, and stomped across the mall pavilion and out of sight.

"I would venture to say he is the most temperamental artist in the area," the board president said, and everyone laughed.

Everyone but Shandra. She had feared his anger when she'd found fault with his piece. So much so, she'd discussed putting it in the exhibition with both Ryan and Leilani. But they had told her she couldn't compromise the exhibit's excellence by pandering to a temperament. She'd agreed.

Now she found herself being surrounded by the artists who were in the exhibition.

"Can you believe the tantrum Patrick threw?" Elijah Lee, an artist in the show, asked. His piece was an oil painting of a surfer and turtle riding a wave. The joy on both faces and movement of the water had struck Shandra with the young man's talent.

"He's been working hard to bring out his craft," Jonas Nakamura, another artist, said. He was a seasoned artist who had two paintings in the exhibit. Both nature scenes. One in oil and one in water colors.

"He's the most sensitive artist I've ever come across," Celia Niau, a ceramic artist, said. "He is gifted. I don't understand why he brought that piece to be juried." This artist had created a delicate rendition of a coral reef. The creation had made Shandra feel as if she were swimming in the reef.

The woman's statement caught Shandra's attention. "He has better pieces?"

"Yes. At least a dozen that show emotion and

movement. I don't understand why he brought that one." Celia clutched the shiny shell on her necklace.

Saul Southwell, a multi-media artist around the same age as Patrick, scoffed. "Everything he paints is dull and boring. We all know that."

Shandra studied the man. His tone wasn't so much patronizing as wishful. Did the creator of an abstract scene of trash and oil on a beach think Patrick had more talent than him?

"He's up and down all the time," Mr. Darnell, the board president, said. "Last week he turned down a scholarship I offered him after he said he'd take it the week before."

The slight raising of eyebrows and knowing gazes caught Shandra's attention. What did the artistic community know about the board president's scholarships?

"You're all being mean talking about Patrick when he isn't here to defend himself." Billie Moon, a potter whose gourd shape vases played on Shandra's weakness for the shapes, stood up for the artist who'd fled. "He has been going through a trying time." She faced Shandra. "This exhibit meant everything to him. Having that painting on display…" Tears glinted in her eyes. She spun around and walked away.

Ryan joined Shandra. "Ready to go?"

"Can Leilani leave now?" She glanced over at her friend who was in a conversation with Billie.

"She gave me the keys to her place and said she'd be there in a couple hours." Ryan excused them from the group.

"See you Friday night at the Opening Reception," Helen Ventura, a bark cloth weaver, said.

Shandra Higheagle Mystery Books

Double Duplicity

Tarnished Remains

Deadly Aim

Murderous Secrets

Killer Descent

Reservation Revenge

Yuletide Slaying

Fatal Fall

Haunting Corpse

Artful Murder

Dangerous Dance

Homicide Hideaway

Toxic Trigger-point

"Yes. I'll be here. See you then." Shandra couldn't shake the effect Patrick's disappointment had embedded in her. She knew all about trying to get recognition for months and sometimes years of work.

"Come on. I thought we'd go for a walk on the beach before turning in." Ryan led her out to the rental car, drove her through the tree tunnel road to Kōloa, and through the town to Poʻipū Beach.

Shandra smiled. Growing up she'd never seen the ocean, but as an adult, once she'd experienced the muted thunder of the waves, the spray of the salt water, tang in the air, and had her feet cradled in the soft, crunching sand, she was hooked. A walk on the beach was what she needed after the confrontation with Patrick.

"You know me so well," she said, stepping out of the rental car and grasping Ryan's hand.

"After the way that guy treated everyone at the gallery, I figured you could use the calming effects of the ocean, sand," he pointed upwards, "and moonlight."

She leaned her head on his shoulder as they walked out onto the beach. "This is perfect." A sigh escaped before she breathed in the damp air tinted with fish, salt, and Ryan's aftershave. Nothing could have been better.

They meandered along the beach at the water line. The soft warm sand cushioned her steps. The crashing of small waves punctuated the quietness of the near empty beach. Moonlight glistened on the water giving the feeling they walked under and beside the twinkling night sky.

"We should go to the house. Leilani will think we got lost driving back." Shandra stared out at the vastness of the ocean and up at the stars and moon, before leading Ryan to the parked car.

Between the two of them, they found their way back to Leilani's house.

"She's not home yet," Shandra said, a bit surprised. Her friend had been the quintessential host. Keeping them fed, showing them the sights, and making sure Shandra was everywhere she needed to be on time.

"She said she'd be a couple hours," Ryan said, unlocking the door.

"There was nothing to do but turn off the lights and lock the doors. I doubt anyone stayed around, there weren't any refreshments. Friday is when everyone will mingle." She didn't know why, but the same dread that had settled in her stomach before talking to Patrick had returned.

Chapter Two

Shandra couldn't sleep. The Grandfather clock leaning up against the wall in Leilani's formal dining room bonged midnight. Her friend had yet to come home. The event ended four hours ago. Where could she be?

The light on the stairway went on, and Ryan lumbered down the stairs. His half-open eyes widened when his feet hit the floor.

She sat in the chair at the bottom of the stairs.

"What are you doing sitting down here in the dark?" he asked.

"Waiting for Leilani. I'm worried." She stood and followed her husband into the kitchen.

He switched on the lights and rummaged in the refrigerator. "What are you worried about?"

"Patrick was so angry when he left…" She didn't want to say her worry out loud. Fear for her friend had been swimming in her stomach all night.

"He was angry with nearly everyone there. He just aimed it at Leilani because she was near the door." Ryan pulled out a bowl of fresh fruit, placing it on the counter. He grabbed two bowls and started dishing up the pineapple, mango, and bananas.

Light flickered through the kitchen window.

"There she is. Now don't go interrogating her. Us staying here as long as we have may have put a cramp in her love life," Ryan said, wiggling his eyebrows.

Shandra smiled and shook her head. "Leave it to a man to think that way."

"What?" He acted offended, and she laughed.

The door from the garage into the kitchen opened. Leilani's dress was torn. Her hair had fallen out of the soft braid that had cascaded down her front right side. Her hands and knees were scratched and bleeding. She was barefoot.

Shandra hurried over to her friend. "What happened?"

The woman stared at Shandra. "I-I went to explain-to—He fell. I-I tried to…" Tears trickled down the sides of her face.

Ryan stepped up to the two of them. "Who fell? Where?"

Sorrow pinched Leilani's face. "Patrick. At his studio."

"Did you call the police?" Ryan was all business now.

"I-I…"

He grabbed Leilani by the shoulders and made her look at him. "Did you call the police?"

"I tried to climb down to him, but I realized I couldn't get down that far." She shoved her hair out of her face.

"Did you call anyone?" Shandra asked, more gently than her husband.

Leilani shook her head. "I got in my car and drove here. But there were lights at his studio."

"Call the police," Ryan said. "I'm going to change and drive out there. You stay here with Leilani."

Shandra pulled Leilani's phone out of her purse and dialed 9-1-1. "I'd like to report an accident. A man fell over a cliff." She asked Leilani. "Where at?"

"Halekoa Point. But they'll find him... Oh, I think I'm going to be sick." Leilani ran into the bathroom off the entryway.

Shandra relayed the message.

Ryan bounded down the stairs, dressed and dangling the car keys. "Where am I headed?"

"Halekoa Point. Be careful." Shandra squeezed his arm as he reached for the door knob.

"Always. Take care of Leilani. I'll call as soon as I know something." Ryan kissed her and disappeared out the door.

Shandra stood outside the bathroom door listening to her friend cry.

~*~

Ryan put the point into his GPS and followed the directions across town to a dirt road until he came to a T. Here the GPS told him to stop. Seeing flashing lights to his right, he eased the rental car that direction and spotted a small building sitting in the middle of nowhere. The activity was to the right of the small building.

Parking his vehicle out of the way of the official ones, he got out and walked over to where several people, including two in uniform, were staring down over the side of the cliff.

"What happened?" he asked the closest person.

"Someone's over the edge," the reply came from a familiar voice.

Ryan peered into the dim backlight from the rescuer's spotlights. Judging from the height and slender build, he thought it was one of the artists from the exhibition. What would he be doing out here this time of night?

Easing himself closer, Ryan had a better look at the man. It was the painter close to Patrick's age who'd made a less than complimentary comment.

"Who's over the edge?" Ryan asked.

"Since this is Patrick James' studio, I'd guess it would be him."

The smirk in the man's tone caught Ryan's attention. "How did anyone know he fell? Was he the only one here?"

"Why are you asking so many questions," a deep voice behind Ryan asked.

He glanced over his shoulder and couldn't miss the massive body standing behind him. "Curious."

The man put a large hand on his shoulder, spinning him around. "Curiosity killed the cat. Did you help Patrick over the cliff?"

Ryan put up his hands. "Not me. I heard about it and came to see if it was true."

"Who did you hear about it from?" The man walked him over into the light. Which glinted off a badge sticking out of the man's shirt pocket.

Slipping his hand into his pocket, Ryan pulled out his badge. Not to butt in, only to let the man know he was a policeman as well.

"The woman my wife and I are staying with—"

"Leilani did this! Man, I thought there was something going on," The voice of the artist grew closer as the man walked into the light.

"Nothing's going on—" Ryan started.

"Leilani who?" the man, obviously a detective asked.

"Sir, can we—"

"It's Detective *Ka-neh*." The man emphasized how to say his name. "Leilani who?" He crossed his arms and stared.

"Leilani Brown." The irritating artist said.

"Where can I find her?" The detective continued to watch Ryan.

He rattled off the address. "My wife is there with her now. We're the ones who called this in."

The officer shook his head. "You may have called it in, but there were three calls."

Men carrying a gurney basket appeared over the top of the cliff.

Ryan stared at the tarped body, wondering who else had called. The person who did it? Someone who was watching and would say they saw Leilani here. And then there was his wife's friend. It wasn't looking good for the Exhibition chairperson.

He scanned the area. A small building was lit up like a lighthouse. "Is that his studio?"

"Yeah. Maybe your wife will find something in there worthy of being in the art exhibition." The artist walked away, laughing.

"What was that about?" Detective Kane asked.

Ryan explained why he and Shandra were in

Kaua'i and how the victim, if it were Patrick James, had been upset when he left the gathering earlier in the evening.

"Leilani Brown. Was she upset with him?" The detective had his logbook out, writing in it.

Ryan shook his head. "I was standing beside her. She appeared sad, but not angry or upset."

"Go back to her place. As soon as I get confirmation it is this Patrick, I'll be over to see Ms. Brown and your wife."

Chapter Three

This night was becoming longer and longer.
Shandra sat in the living room, her feet curled up under
her on the sofa. Ryan sat beside her. Leilani had
showered and changed by the time Ryan returned and
told them a Detective Kane would be coming by
shortly.

The doorbell rang.

Leilani didn't move.

Ryan squeezed Shandra's leg and went to the door.

"Just tell the truth," she said in a quiet voice to
Leilani as the men's voices grew closer.

"This is my wife, Shandra," Ryan said, motioning
to her.

She stood and shook the detective's hand. He was a
big man. Tall, broad, with large hands and feet. His
round face under short-cropped black hair was as
inquisitive as it was stern.

Detective Kane's gaze skipped over Shandra to

study Leilani. He released her hand and pulled a chair up to the one where Leilani sat.

Shandra grasped Ryan's hand, and they sat down on the sofa. She leaned to Ryan and whispered, "Was it Patrick?" She had hoped it wasn't. If he'd jumped off the cliff because of her words… She held onto Ryan's hand for stability.

He nodded.

"Ms. Brown. What were you doing at Halekoa Point tonight?" the detective asked.

Leilani didn't look up from the pillow where her fingers picked at the fringe. "Was the man I saw fall over the cliff Patrick?" she asked.

"You saw him fall?" The detective yanked a logbook from his pocket.

She wiped at a tear trickling down the side of her face with the heel of one hand and nodded. "After I cleaned up from the event at the gallery, I drove to his studio. I wanted to make sure he didn't ruin his other work."

Shandra sat up. "What do you mean?"

Detective Kane frowned at her.

Leilani glanced up. "I learned after the fact, that about six months ago, when he'd not made it into a juried show, he'd gone to his studio and trashed the other pieces of art he had painted." She hugged the pillow to her. "When Celia said he had better work at the studio than he'd brought to be in the exhibition, I didn't want him ruining months of work."

"Where were you when you saw the victim fall off the cliff?" Detective Kane asked.

Her friend's head snapped around. She stared at the detective as if she'd forgotten he was there. "What?"

"Where were you when the victim fell off the cliff?"

"I had gone into his studio. I was relieved to see he hadn't destroyed anything. But wondered where he could be. The light had been on when I walked in. His motorcycle was parked behind the building." She closed her eyes. "It all feels like a dream."

"It wasn't a dream Ms. Brown. How did you know it was the victim who fell?" The detective studied Leilani.

"I wasn't sure. I thought I heard him call out to me. I flicked the light off so I could see in the dark better. I saw someone near the edge of the cliff and called out." She continued, her eyes closed, hands twisted together. "When he started teetering, I ran, but he fell before I got there. I tried to climb down to him, but realized, he'd gone farther down than I could climb in the dark."

The detective didn't move. "Why didn't you call for help from there? Why drive all the way back here?"

Leilani stared at him.

"I think she was in shock," Shandra cut in. "She was incoherent and unseeing when she walked into the house."

"I've seen many people use that ploy to avoid answering questions," Detective Kane said.

Shandra opened her mouth to object when Ryan's hand rested on her leg to keep her quiet. She studied her friend. The collected woman who had run this event with such competence looked unable to write her own name.

"Ms. Brown, why didn't you call from the point? Why did you drive all the way back here?" Detective Kane asked.

Leilani didn't look up. "My phone was in my car. In my purse. When I sat down in the seat, all I could think about was getting home. I forgot to call, I just wanted to be home. Where I was safe."

Shandra studied her friend. Had she seen more than Patrick falling off the cliff?

"Safe?" The detective grabbed onto that phrase as well. "Didn't you feel safe at the point?"

Her head moved back and forth slowly. "No. When I crawled back up the cliff, I felt as if someone was watching. Then I thought, what if it was whoever caused Patrick to fall." She wrapped her arms tighter around the pillow.

Shandra's gaze traveled to the detective. He wasn't buying this. She could tell by his furrowed brow and pursed lips. "Did you see someone with Patrick when you first saw him?"

Leilani peered at Shandra. She shook her head. "No. Not really. I mean it was dark. I'd just been inside the studio in the light and I'd looked outside."

"You said you turned the lights off." The detective placed the point of his pen on a section of the logbook page.

"I did. I remember doing that. But the lights were on when I went to my car." Her eyes widened. "Someone else was there!"

"Or, you went to see the victim, he was still angry with you, you argued, and he went over the cliff."

"But her dress was torn, her knees and hands are scratched—" As soon as the words came out, Shandra knew she'd said too much. She glanced at Ryan. He nodded. She should have known, if she hadn't said anything, he would have. The police needed all the evidence.

Detective Kane slid to the edge of his seat. "Let me see your hands, *ke 'olu 'olu*."

Leilani held her hands out, showing her palms and the backs.

The detective pulled out his phone and took photos. "Your knees."

She obediently pulled the legs of her sweatpants up above her knees.

Detective Kane took photos of her knees and said, "What about the clothes?"

"I'll get them," Shandra said, standing.

"Don't do anything stupid," the detective said.

Chapter Four

Shandra left the room after throwing a scowl towards Detective Kane. Ryan knew his wife wouldn't do anything stupid and it insulted him that this man would think such a thing.

"My wife knows not to tamper with evidence," he said, glaring at the other man.

"It's been my experience that even the most law-abiding will try to 'help' friends and family in a situation like this and it usually tends to muck up the water." The detective shoved back in the chair, watching Leilani.

"Does this look like a suicide?" Ryan asked.

The woman shuddered, and the detective glanced at him sideways.

"I'm not at liberty to discuss the preliminary findings."

"Come on. As one police officer to another. You have to have some thoughts on this. Did you know the victim? Had he been in trouble with the law?" Ryan knew he was pushing, considering this was a long way from his jurisdiction.

"Here you go. I used a towel to put them in the garbage sack." Shandra returned with a bulging fourteen-gallon wastebasket liner.

"*Mahalo*." Detective Kane stood, took the bag, and headed for the door.

"Any chance if I came to your police station tomorrow, I could learn a bit more about this incident?" Ryan followed the man to the door and out to the patrol car. He knew Shandra would be shoving her nose into the investigation because her friend was involved.

"This is for the Kaua'i Police to take care of. Not an off-islander."

"Kane, you don't understand. My wife is going to want to help her friend. And if I don't get the information from you, she is going to get in your way." He didn't want to come out and say his wife, a layman, had a pretty good conviction rate.

"She's your *wahine*, keep her out of it." Kane opened the car door.

Ryan held onto the door. "You don't understand. It's not that easy. But since you aren't willing to cooperate, I will let you know what she digs up." He had no choice. Her grandmother would come to her in dreams, and they would both be neck deep in this. Shandra wouldn't give up until she'd found the person who caused the victim to fall off the cliff.

"I said keep her out of it." Kane levered his tall frame into the vehicle.

"It's not that easy." Ryan shut the door and watched the police vehicle back out of the drive.

In the house, Shandra sat on the stool in front of Leilani's chair. "You need to get your sleep. You and the other board members will need to decide whether or not to continue with the Opening Reception on Friday night."

Leilani sat up. "Oh no! Someone has to contact all the board members and call a meeting."

"We'll do that in the morning. Come on." Shandra helped her friend to her feet and led her upstairs.

Ryan couldn't think of anything else they could do with what was left of the night. He followed them up the stairs, turning off the lights.

~*~

After Shandra coerced Leilani into eating some breakfast, they phoned the board members and called an emergency meeting for one that afternoon.

Shandra was pleased all the board members expected her to be at the meeting. She wanted to know more about Brendan Darnell's scholarship that the victim accepted then declined. And she wanted to know who, besides the artists she'd met, was close to Patrick.

"I think I'll wander down to the police station and see if anyone will talk to me while you and Leilani attend the board meeting," Ryan said, when their host went up to her room to get dressed.

"I don't think the detective who was here last night will let you snoop around in his investigation," Shandra said, pouring fresh coffee into Ryan's cup.

"I'm pretty sure he won't either. But I might be able to learn something anyway."

She kissed him. "You can be very persuasive when you want to."

As soon as Ryan left, Shandra headed to the room

they occupied, and dressed. When she returned to the kitchen, Leilani stood at the window staring out at the street.

"Patrick's death isn't your fault or mine," Shandra said.

The woman jumped and spun around, facing her. "It is my fault. I knew how fragile his ego was. When he brought that hideous painting in, I should have suggested he go home and get one of his better works."

Shandra studied her friend. "You knew he had better paintings? How? Why did you let him enter the one he did?"

Leilani wrung her hands and stared at the floor. "There was something about Patrick. Ask any of the women who were at the exhibition last night. When he wasn't in his moods, he was charming, charismatic." She flicked a glance up then back to the floor. "He made a woman feel beautiful and loved."

"You and Patrick were lovers?" Shandra could see Detective Kane discovering this and thinking Leilani and Patrick had a lover's spat. In the heat of the argument, she'd shoved him off the cliff.

"Not in the sense of anything long term happening. He had his sights on someone else, and I didn't want people thinking I was robbing the cradle." Leilani shoved her dark hair behind an ear and peered at Shandra. "I didn't kill him. I went there to make sure he didn't do something stupid. When he got in his moods, it was like he was in a daze and afterwards wouldn't remember what he'd done."

Shandra had another thought. "Which of the women at the event last night were also his lovers?" One of them could have gone to Patrick thinking the same thing as Leilani.

Leilani smiled wanly. "Just about every woman there except Billie and you. He was a favorite in the art community. The women loved him and the men thought of him as a temperamental brother."

"I heard some comments last night that didn't sound like he was so well thought of." Shandra remembered specifically, the multi-media artist. "Saul hadn't anything flattering to say about Patrick."

"They had a falling out over that damn scholarship Brendan offered Patrick." She made a weird sound in her throat. "As if Patrick would take a scholarship from Brendan." Leilani seemed to be shaking off her guilt as she talked about the artists in her community. "There are stipulations that go with Brendan's scholarships. Some artists are willing to follow them in order to be able to work on their craft full time without having to also juggle a job, while others are smart enough to not accept. That was Patrick. Brendan had offered Patrick a scholarship every year for the last three years. That made Saul mad. He would have done anything Brendan asked if he had been offered the chance. Not Patrick. While he was temperamental, he was also very proud."

Shandra was interested in the stipulations. "What did the artists have to do if they accepted Brendan's scholarship?"

"Be at his beck and call. If it happened to be a female artist, she had to be ready to be his date at a moment's notice. And I heard, he even had sex with some of them." Leilani's body shook in distaste. "As for the males. The same beck and call, but usually to fill in for card parties, sports, and other odd jobs Brendan came up with." Her brow furrowed. "If you ask me it would be demeaning to have to do all of that for the man just to have the money to work on what you loved."

"I'm surprised anyone would want his scholarship, knowing all of that." Shandra had felt unsettled around the board member from the first time she'd met him. Now she realized it was because he used people, much like her now deceased first lover.

"You'd be surprised how many starving artists are on this island, and willing to take his twenty-thousand dollars no matter what."

Shandra whistled. "I didn't realize it was that much money."

"And they move into the small cottage on his estate and don't have to pay any of the utilities. Just purchase their food and art supplies." Leilani ran her hands through her hair. "It is something that is hard to pass up when you are starting out."

Shandra studied her friend. "Did you use his scholarship?"

"I was getting ready to accept when Helen told me to reconsider and mentioned the last woman who had accepted found herself pregnant, and Brendan refused to acknowledge the baby was his." Anger darkened her friend's cheeks. "There is nothing lower than a man who won't own up to the human he created."

From their acquaintance in college, Shandra knew that had been the case of Leilani's birthfather.

"We better go grab lunch and meet the board," Shandra suggested, thinking there could be any number of people who might have shoved Patrick off the cliff, if he'd been shoved. With his moods and ego, they still couldn't rule out suicide.

Chapter Five

Ryan stood inside the Līhuʻe Police Station visiting with the desk sergeant when Detective Kane walked through the door from the interior of the building.

"What are you doing here? I said we didn't need off island help." The detective stopped three feet from Ryan and crossed his arms.

"I just wanted to buy you a cup of coffee." Ryan nodded toward the outside door.

Kane studied him several seconds before letting out a huff and relaxing his arms. "I have fifteen minutes."

The man was giving in. Ryan hoped it was because the detective was willing to allow him access to the case and not just to get him off his back.

Out on the sidewalk, Ryan stared at the isolated area of the police and court buildings. "Where do you go for a cup of coffee not brewed in the station?"

Kane walked over to an unmarked car. "Follow me."

Ryan slipped behind the steering wheel of the rental car and followed the policeman out of the parking lot, onto a main road, and past a stadium. They turned right and were soon in the business district. The police car stopped in front of a coffee shop.

One parking spot was available three cars beyond the police vehicle. Ryan pulled in and parked. Kane was already disappearing into the building when Ryan stepped out of the car.

Inside, the big man held two coffees in his hands when he turned from the counter. Ryan found an empty table away from the half a dozen other coffee drinkers.

When they were seated, Kane started. "Why are you so interested in this artist's death? Is there something you aren't telling me about your connection to him?"

Ryan sipped his coffee. It was strong. Placing the cup on the table, he studied the detective. "We, my wife and I, had never met the victim until the day the art was brought to the mall gallery. She and I watched the artists bring their things in, she briefly talked to them, and then we left. The night he died was only the second time we'd seen the man. It was an event where my wife, being the juror for the show, explained why she picked the exhibits she did and why the others didn't make it."

"And the victim's painting didn't make it into the exhibition?" Kane picked up his coffee.

"That's right. My wife tried to explain diplomatically why his painting didn't make the show. He exploded. Shouted at several people and stormed out of the building with his painting."

The man raised a brow. "He threatened both your

wife and the woman you are staying with, I heard."

"He threatened everyone in the place. He wasn't acting rationally." Ryan thought back to the night. Leilani had seemed upset by Patrick's words to her. Was it because she feared him or because she feared what he would do to his art, as she'd said?

"How well do you know Ms. Brown?" Detective Kane asked.

"She's a college friend of my wife. Until coming here, I had never met the woman." Was he using Shandra's belief in someone she knew to blind him from the facts? The woman had looked as if she'd struggled with someone, and one or both of them, fell down the side of the cliff.

"What did you find that implicates Ms. Brown?"

When the detective just stared at him, Ryan added, "I want to know if I need to move my wife out of the house of a killer."

"We haven't established Ms. Brown as the murderer, but she is a person of interest."

"Why? Because she didn't call the police right away?"

The man didn't twitch.

"She was in a state of shock."

"That could be because she'd just wrestled with a man who fell to his death." Detective Kane raised his coffee and took a sip.

"Did the fall kill him?" Ryan wondered if the man had been lying down the cliff injured but not dead and could have been helped if proper authorities had been called.

"I'll tell you this. The fall didn't kill him, but it made him unable to ward off the blow that did kill him." Kane raised his eyebrows. "Did Ms. Brown get all scratched and her clothing torn trying to save him or to make sure he didn't say she caused his fall?"

~*~

Shandra sat in the small back room of the makeshift art gallery at the mall. There were six people, counting herself, sitting in chairs around a small table. Brendan Darnell was the last to arrive. Shandra had been pleased the seats on either side of her were taken. After what she'd learned about the man, she would have had a hard time not flinching every time he moved.

"It's a damn shame about Patrick," Brendan said, taking a seat across from Leilani.

"As the board of this exhibition, we need to decide whether to close the doors and call a halt to the activities around the exhibition or to continue," Leilani said, her gaze landing on each person present.

"I say we vote," Mrs. Graham, an art teacher at one of the high schools, said.

"By hand or secret vote?" Mr. Blanc asked. He had been introduced as the manager of the bank sponsoring the event.

"I say secret ballet, so no one feels intimidated to vote one way or the other," Mrs. Kim, a wealthy benefactor, said.

Shandra agreed. She'd already discerned how the other people at the table felt about Brendan. She didn't want them seeing his vote and voting the opposite out of spite. She studied the woman and realized she had the same thoughts.

"That's a good idea." Leilani said. "And since Shandra makes us even and is the juror and not part of the organization, she'll pass out the paper and pens and collect the votes."

Shandra nodded. It made sense to her, and she was torn about whether the event should go on. But this was something these people held every year. It was their opinion that mattered and not hers.

She found a blank paper, cut it into five even pieces and handed those and pens to the five at the table. Standing back, she said, "Either write yes to continue or no to stop the exhibition."

Once everyone set their pens down, she gathered the slips and handed them to Leilani.

Her friend unfolded the first paper. "Yes."

The second. "No."

The third. "No."

The fourth. "Yes."

"It's two to two. This last one will decide what we do." She opened it and said, "Yes."

The others at the table glanced around.

"I think we should hold the event in honor of Patrick," Brendan said.

Leilani's gaze bore into the man. "Why this year? I think to best show our support to his art, we should rename the event after him next year."

Several others muttered their agreement.

Anger flashed in the man's eyes before he stood. "It's settled. We continue as usual. Renaming the event can come up at the next meeting." He stalked out of the room. There was a collective releasing of breath. What did that man have over all of these people? Shandra studied each one. Something she'd look into when they were back at Leilani's.

"It was wonderful meeting you," Mrs. Graham

said. "We'll talk more on Friday night at the opening of the exhibition."

Shandra nodded and watched as the other board members left the room.

Leilani remained seated. "You don't think any of them know I was at Patrick's when it happened, do you?"

"I'm pretty sure Brendan knows. It was the way he looked at you. But the others, no." Shandra walked to the door. "Come on, let's go home and see what Ryan found out."

Leilani didn't stand. "Do you really think going on with the exhibition is the right thing to do?"

Shandra sat back down. "Do you think the artists should be asked, too? After all, it will be their work people are coming to see."

"They will all say to go on with the event. They know the promotion that has been done and the prestige that comes from being an artist picked for this exhibition. They wouldn't want to lose that or a possible sale by shutting it down." Leilani stared at the table top. "I should have gotten there sooner. I could tell when he left, he was upset. Really upset."

"Short of having been on the edge of the cliff, talking him out of it, there was nothing you could do." Shandra stood and tugged at her friend's arm. "Come on."

"That's it. He wasn't jumping. I swear something caused him to fall. Like he tripped at the edge." Leilani peered at her. "If I had been out there with him at the edge of the cliff, I might have been able to keep him from going over."

Chapter Six

The house was quiet when they returned. Shandra pulled out her phone and texted Ryan. *Where are you? Can we go look at Patrick's Studio?*

Ten away. Was his replied text.

She opened her phone to a search engine and put in Brendan Darnell, Līhu'e, Hawaii. The man's family had raised sugar cane before selling their holdings to the family that now had a large coffee plantation on the island. Which left Brendan a rich man with nothing to do but stick his fingers in many non-profit organizations.

Knowing what she did about his Art Scholarship, she already didn't like the man. Could he have been hidden along the edge and shoved or pulled Patrick to his death? But why?

The doorbell rang.

Shandra shook off her thoughts and answered.

Ryan stood on the step.

She pulled him inside. "Well, did you learn anything else?"

He held up a hand. "Why do you want to see the studio?"

"Curiosity. I want to see if he had paintings that were better than the one he put in the exhibition." And she wanted to see the scene of the crime. But she wasn't going to tell him that.

"You know that will most likely be sealed off. I'm not sure I've made that good of a buddy with Detective Kane."

Shandra laughed. "But you are on speaking terms?"

"He bought me coffee and I learned the fall didn't kill Patrick."

Shandra shuddered.

A gasp sounded from the stairway. Leilani held a hand over her mouth, her eyes wide, and her face pale.

Shandra hurried to her friend, helping her the rest of the way down the stairs.

Leilani plopped into the chair. "You're saying if I had called as soon as I saw him fall, he would still be alive?"

Ryan studied her friend. Shandra had a bad feeling her husband hadn't crossed Leilani off the list of suspects.

"I'm saying, if he slipped or was pushed, whoever saw or did it, went down and finished him off."

Ryan's blunt words froze Shandra's insides. Someone had purposely killed the artist. She didn't believe her friend had, however, she continued to study the woman.

Leilani's eyes widened as her gaze bounced back

and forth between Shandra and Ryan. "You two think…Oh no! Is that what that policeman thinks too?"

Shandra dropped to her knees beside her friend's chair. "No, I don't think you did it. I'm worried whoever did, might think you saw something."

Leilani's body visibly shook. "I-I didn't. After going down the cliff about ten feet, I realized it was useless to get to him."

"Think. Did you hear anything? A cry from Patrick? The sound of someone else moving about?" Ryan's voice was soft and low as he asked.

Leilani's head vibrated back and forth. "The pounding of my head, my heart. The roar of waves." She closed her eyes. "I slipped backwards once. Rocks slid out from under my feet." Her eyes opened. "I heard a ping. Like a rock hit metal."

Shandra glanced at her husband. His brow was furrowed in thought.

"Will you be okay alone?" Shandra asked. "Ryan and I are going out to drive around and see some more sights."

Leilani sniffed. "Yes, go. I don't plan to leave my house until Opening night. You should enjoy more beaches. Go north to Hanalei. There are pretty beaches that way."

"You're sure you'll be okay?" Shandra asked, not wanting to sound like she was in a hurry to get away from the shattered woman.

"I'm fine. Go enjoy." Leilani stood and pulled a tissue from a container on the entryway table.

"I'll go grab our swimsuits," Shandra said, dashing up the stairs.

~*~

Ryan studied the area where the paramedics brought up the body the night before as he parked the car over by the studio. Forensics were still milling about. A glance at the studio revealed crime tape across the door. "I don't think you're going to get a chance to look at the art in the studio."

"You can go visit with the people over there while I figure out a way in."

Ryan shook his head. "You aren't going in there without an invitation by the police."

Shandra stared at him. "You know I won't disturb anything."

"I know that, but if you get caught, the police here will think you're tampering with evidence." Ryan motioned for them to get out of the rental. He met her at the front of the vehicle and grasped her hand. "Let's go see who is in charge and visit with them a bit."

"Do you think Detective Kane will be here?" Shandra asked.

"He didn't say anything like that when we visited earlier." However, Ryan had a feeling the man would find out if they entered the studio. And that was why he wanted to make sure they had someone's permission.

"Hey, you need to stay back." An officer in uniform who had been staring down the cliff as they approached, turned to them.

"Have you learned anything new?" Ryan asked, flashing his badge so fast the man wouldn't have a chance to see what department was on it.

"They are finding lots of trash. Maybe a couple things that might pertain to the case." The officer glanced at Shandra. "You a cop, too?"

"No. She's here to look over the art in the studio."

"You think this guy was painting fakes?" the man had his full attention on Shandra.

"We just want to rule out everything," she said, being non-committal.

Ryan would have groaned, but he didn't want the officer to realize they shouldn't be here.

"I can walk you over and unlock the door." The officer strode toward the studio. "Didn't know this guy myself. My sister said she'd read a story about him in the paper a while back."

Ryan filed that away. He'd like to know what the paper had to say about the victim.

"He was an up-and-coming artist," Shandra said.

Ryan glanced at her to see if she said it without wincing. He knew she hadn't thought the young man had much talent given the one piece she'd seen.

At the door, the officer pulled down the tape at one side and unlocked the door. "Be sure to lock back up and re-stick this tape when you finish."

"We will," Ryan said, hoping Kane didn't press charges against them if he found out.

Shandra moseyed into the studio, her gaze traveling slowly over the interior. "He kept a tidy studio."

Ryan studied the glasses sitting on a small end table between two cushioned chairs. It appeared he'd had company last night. It would have been before Leilani arrived. Or it was she and the victim having drinks before taking a walk and the victim falling to his death. He frowned. Why hadn't forensics taken the glasses away? They would have photographed the building already.

"Look at these," Shandra said, standing by a stack

of paintings leaning against a wall. She had a rag in both hands as she flipped through the paintings.

"That's nice," he said, studying a small alcove with a sailboat bouncing in the waves off shore. "Why didn't he put this one in the show?"

"That's what I'm wondering. Any of these would have made it into the exhibition had he brought them." She pivoted from looking at the paintings and scanned the room. "Where is the painting that he entered?" She moved blank canvases peering behind them. "Do you think the police took it?"

Ryan shook his head. "But they didn't take the two glasses sitting on the table."

Shandra spun to the table and frowned. "Why not?"

"Because we didn't expect people to come snooping about."

Chapter Seven

The voice sounded disappointed. Shandra pivoted to the door, knowing they had been caught by Detective Kane. This would look bad for Ryan and could get them both booted so far from the investigation she couldn't help Leilani.

"Detective Kane, I asked my husband to bring me here…"

"Your husband knows a taped crime scene is off limits." The officer stared at Ryan. "Even if the person has a badge from somewhere else."

"I'm sorry. I wanted to see if Patrick had better paintings than he'd brought to be juried." She waved her hands. "Look around. They are all one hundred percent better than the one he was trying to get put in the show. Why?"

The officer crossed his beefy arms and stared at her. "Are you trying to tell me that he was killed because his painting didn't make the exhibition?"

She shuffled her feet under his intense gaze, but the thought had occurred to her. "He was really upset that the painting didn't make it. And looking at his other work, he knew it wasn't good enough."

"His comment to Leilani, about her keeping him from getting his painting in," Ryan said. "I wonder if she had promised it would be picked. Then when you pushed her about putting it in to not get a tantrum like you did, she said, no, don't cater to his moods." Ryan pointed a finger at Detective Kane. "You might want to ask Ms. Brown if they had made an agreement beforehand that she would make sure his painting was included."

Shandra hadn't said anything to Ryan about what Leilani had told her about the young artist's charisma. Now might be the time with Detective Kane present. "Leilani admitted to me last night that she and Patrick had been lovers."

Detective Kane opened his mouth as if to speak, and she hurriedly continued. "She also said, he had slept with every female artist that was at the event last night, except Billie. It didn't seem to bother her that he slept with any female in the art world. I'm wondering if he did it to get other favors from them? Like him possibly asking Leilani to make sure the painting made it into the exhibit."

"That's stretching things a bit. But it might be the motive for your friend to kill him."

Shandra shook her head. "She didn't do it. I believe her. But I also don't think she's told us everything. Like possibly the painting."

"Did you take it away last night?" she asked Detective Kane.

"Take what away?" he asked.

"The painting." Shandra waved her arms. "It's not here."

The detective shook his head. "We haven't taken anything out of here." He peered at Ryan. "That is why the crime tape is still up. Once Forensics finishes with the cliff, they will come here."

Ryan pointed to the two glasses. "That's why those are still there."

"This is a crime scene. I'd appreciate the two of you getting out and staying out of my investigation." He swooped a hand toward the open door.

Shandra started to protest when Ryan gripped her arm and led her out.

"I wasn't through looking around."

"As far as Detective Kane is concerned, you are finished." Ryan escorted her to the passenger side of the car. "Get in. We'll hash over what we discovered on the way back to Leilani's. She has more questions to answer."

~*~

Back at Leilani's, Shandra was surprised to see cars lined up along the street in front of her friend's house.

"Who do you think is here?" Shandra asked Ryan as they walked up to the front door.

He shrugged and rang the doorbell.

Leilani answered, her face reddened when she saw them. "Oh! You two are back soon. I thought you were going to enjoy the northern beaches."

Shandra had a feeling they weren't supposed to know about whoever was here. "We were at Patrick's studio looking at his art work."

Ryan had already moved past them into the living room.

Shandra followed and discovered the women Leilani had alluded to having all slept with the deceased.

"We were discussing how to go about getting next year's exhibition named after Patrick," her friend said before anyone else could say a word.

The rise of Ryan's eyebrow revealed he didn't believe her either.

"I'm glad you are all here," Shandra said, taking a seat. "What can you tell me about the painting Patrick wanted in the exhibition?"

"What do you mean?" Celia asked, glancing at the other women present. A couple of them were artists whose work hadn't made the cut for the exhibition.

"I just saw the work Patrick had at his studio. Any one of those would have made the show. Why did he pick or paint that one specifically for the show?"

Billie, who according to Leilani, was the only woman who hadn't slept with Patrick, spoke up, "When I asked him why he was putting that poor quality work in the exhibition, he said he'd been promised it would make the show."

Leilani's face reddened.

"But why did he want that specific painting?" Ryan chimed in.

The young woman shook her head. "I don't know. But he worked on it longer than on any other painting. I told him his other paintings showed more emotion and heart."

Shandra agreed with that statement. "When did he start working on the one for the exhibition?"

Billie shrugged. The other women murmured amongst themselves.

"Any idea?" Ryan asked.

"I guess a couple months ago." Leilani said, finally. "I mean, that's when he started acting different."

"Different?" Shandra glanced around at the others. They all nodded.

"It was after Mr. Darnell offered him the scholarship," Billie said.

Helen's face paled. "Oh, my goodness!"

"What?" Shandra glanced at Ryan, wondering what the woman would say.

"I told Patrick not to accept the scholarship. I knew he needed money to continue, but I didn't want him becoming that man's slave. It would have syphoned all of Patrick's creativity away."

"What is she talking about? Scholarship?" Ryan studied his wife. It was apparent she hadn't told him everything she'd learned from Leilani. First the information she'd given Detective Kane and now, this.

"I forgot to tell you what Leilani told me about Mr. Darnell's scholarships." Shandra didn't seem the least bit guilty that she'd forgotten to clue him in on the information she'd gathered.

"Let me," Leilani said. "Mr. Darnell puts stipulations on his scholarship."

"Yeah, you have to be his slave in all ways if you accept it," Celia said, bitterness made her words sharp.

Ryan studied the woman. "All ways? You mean sexually?"

"In some cases," Helen said.

"How has he gotten away with that?" Ryan

couldn't fathom an organization that would put up with the likes of Mr. Darnell.

"He does give a generous amount of money to the artist and the use of the cottage on his estate," Celia said.

"But becoming the man's slave for whatever he wants, shouldn't happen," Shandra said.

Ryan knew his wife's past influenced her way of thinking and he agreed. "Why hasn't anyone told the police about this?"

They shrugged.

"Starving artists will do anything to be able to keep working on their art," Celia said.

"When we hear about one of Brendan's scholarships having been issued, we talk to the artist." Helen set down her cup of coffee and stood. "I think we've accomplished all we can at this point."

Ryan stood. "I'm not through."

"What right do you have to detain us?" Helen asked.

"Ryan is a policeman from Idaho. He knows what questions to ask and what information might be vital to this tragedy," Leilani said.

He was thankful the woman seemed to understand he might be able to learn something from the conversation.

"When did Patrick turn down the scholarship?" If he could establish a connection between the artist and the board member, he might be able to see if there was enough animosity between the two that Darnell might have wanted the younger man dead.

"About two months ago, when he started working on that awful painting," Celia said.

"But Mr. Darnell commented last night as if Patrick had just turned him down," Shandra cut in.

"Oh no, it was when Celia said. I was at the studio when Mr. Darnell showed up and asked Patrick if he'd made a decision," Billie said. Her cheeks colored. "I grew up with brothers, but I'd never heard the words that came out of Mr. Darnell's mouth before. Patrick told him to shut up and his mouth was part of the reason he didn't want his scholarship."

"Why would he get so mad that Patrick didn't want the scholarship?" Ryan asked.

All the women but Billie shrugged. He turned his attention to the youngest woman. "Do you know why Darnell wanted Patrick to take the scholarship?"

"I'm not sure. He was yelling something about getting laid and a house full of young women." Confusion wrinkled Billie's face, but the other women's faces held anger. Including his wife's.

"He wanted Patrick to bring young women into his house for his pleasure!" Helen was seething. "He is a pig!" She turned to Leilani. "Is there a way to get him off the board?"

Ryan wasn't sure if the chairman of the Kaua'i Art Society had anything to do with the murder, but he was determined to learn all he could about Brendan Darnell and help the Society keep him from preying on desperate artists.

Chapter Eight

After all the women left, Shandra sat down with Ryan while Leilani cleaned the dishes in the kitchen. "Do you think Brendan Darnell killed Patrick?"

"I don't know. He sounds more like a sleaze than a killer but some people can be pushed, as we well know."

Shandra nodded, since her grandmother started coming to her in dreams and giving her clues to over a dozen murders, she'd learned the killer wasn't always the most logical person.

Ryan picked up her laptop that had been setting on the end table beside the couch.

"Who are you looking up?" she asked, having a pretty good idea.

"Let's see if we can find anything in the local papers about Darnell. And I don't mean the society pages." He raised his eyebrows, and she understood he meant in the police reports or stories.

They'd been digging through the last two years of the newspaper when Leilani walked into the room.

"What are you two looking up?" she asked.

"Do you know if Brendan has ever been in trouble with the law?" Shandra asked.

Her friend shook her head. "I haven't heard anything. But then his cousin is a judge."

Ryan's head popped up from where he'd been browsing the screen. "A judge? What kind?"

Leilani stared at him. "Isn't there only one kind of judge?"

"No, some judges have specific 'expertise' I guess you'd say. Like traffic, courtroom, supreme court."

"Oh, I don't know. His name is James O'Haney." Leilani's gaze landed on the laptop.

Shandra watched as Ryan typed in the name.

Up popped a photo of the man in his judge's robe.

"Criminal," Ryan said, with a distinct connotation that it wasn't good.

"What does that mean?" Leilani asked.

"It means he could clear his cousin of any wrong doing and keep the records sealed." Ryan closed the laptop. "I need to find a fellow lawman that will help me get into files and learn more about the murder."

Leilani sucked in air at his mention of murder. Even though they had told her that before. "Sorry. I just find it hard to believe someone disliked Patrick enough to kill him." She walked over to her purse setting on the table by the front door. She pulled out a card and walked back across the room. "This is my cousin, Jenny Wong. She's a private investigator, but she has ways of finding out things at the police station."

Shandra was surprised Leilani hadn't mentioned

her before. "Does she know you are a suspect in the murder?"

Leilani stared down at her feet. "I didn't tell her, but she called me this morning. Like I said, she has contacts on the police force. I told her I'd be fine because I didn't do it."

"I'm going to call and make a time to go talk to her." Ryan walked out of the room, pulling his phone out of the holster on his belt.

Shandra pulled her friend down beside her on the couch. "I know you're sad about Patrick and the cloud his death has put over the exhibition. But you have to stay positive and help us find who killed him. It's the only way to keep the police from hounding you."

"I understand. I hope Jenny can help Ryan find what he needs." She glanced up from her hands. "Do you really think Brendan killed Patrick?"

"He's just a suspect for us like you are to the police. He may have or he may not but right now, Ryan wants to find information on not only if he was the murderer but also to get him off the Art Society Board. He is a predator and shouldn't have the privilege of finding prey from artists." Her anger grew when she thought of how the man had abused his wealth and status to inure artists to do his bidding.

"Why did you go to Patrick's studio this morning?"

That question was easy to answer. "After everyone said he had better work at his studio, I was curious to see it. But we were caught trespassing by Detective Kane. He kicked us out so I couldn't hunt for the painting I'd rejected. But you were all correct. Any other piece that was in his studio would have made the exhibition list."

Leilani nodded.

"So why did he bring that painting that was obviously not of quality? And according to Billie, he worked on it for two months. That was a lot of time for what he ended up with." She studied her friend. Leilani was deep in thought.

"I agree. He usually finished a painting in less than a week and it would have more detail and dimension than the red one." She threw her hands in the air. "I don't know what was going on in his head. He did ask me to make sure his painting made it into the exhibition." She stared across the room, a sweet smile on her face. "He had me to the studio for dinner one night. He showed me the painting. I questioned it being worthy and said you may not be swayed. He said…" She slapped a hand to her mouth. "I just remembered. He said it was a matter of life or death that the painting be in the show." Tears ran down her cheeks. "I did kill him."

Shandra put an arm around her friend. "No, you didn't kill him. Whatever he was mixed up in killed him."

~*~

Ryan finished his call with Jenny Wong. He was meeting her at the coffee shop he and Detective Kane had visited. Walking into the living room, he found Shandra sitting alone, staring at her laptop.

"Want to meet Leilani's cousin?" he asked.

She smiled, closed the laptop, and stood. "Sounds good. Leilani went to lie down. She's tired and emotionally drained."

He nodded. She'd had a lot happen on her watch as the chairwoman of the art show. "Do you want to let her know where we're going?"

"I'll text her when we get in the car." Shandra picked up her purse and walked to the door ahead of him.

Ryan grinned, following his wife. Since their first meeting when she was a murder suspect, she always pushed to find the truth.

On the way to the coffee shop in Līhu'e, Shandra filled him in on what Leilani had said while he was calling her cousin.

"It sounds like that painting had to be put out in the public." Ryan thought about that. "I wonder if there was something under the painting that was to be given to whoever bought it?"

"I read something like that a few years ago." Shandra pulled out her phone. He heard her clicking the keys, then silence.

"What did you find?" He kept his eyes on the road. There seemed to be more tourists on the island than locals.

"There have been many instances where something is hidden under a painting to smuggle it from country to country." Shandra held her phone up. "What could Patrick have been mixed up in that required his horrific painting to smuggle it?"

"Maybe Jenny will have an idea."

~*~

Walking into the coffee shop, Ryan scanned the room. There were three women sitting alone. One had on a blazer, slacks, and high heels. He doubted a PI in Hawaii would dress like a business woman. That left the other two. One was a woman in her twenties, wearing a tank top, shorts, and flipflops. The other was in her forties, wore Bermuda shorts, a cotton button-up shirt, and athletic shoes without socks.

Before he'd made up his mind, Shandra walked over to the woman in Bermuda shorts.

"Jenny?" she asked, holding out a hand.

"Yes." The woman pulled her gaze from her phone and checked out Shandra before her gaze landed on Ryan. "You didn't say you were bringing backup," Jenny said, winking at Shandra.

"My wife, Shandra," he pulled a chair out for her. "I'll go get us something to drink."

"Cold," Shandra said, sitting.

He had a feeling she would have the woman's history from her by the time he returned with their iced teas.

As he sat back down, Shandra asked Jenny, "How did you become a Private Investigator?"

"I was a cop until a drugged-up homeless person went crazy and killed my partner when we went out on a call of an armed and dangerous woman." Jenny's face held the same blank stare that he'd seen on fellow Army comrades who'd lived through raids and bombings.

She was trying to show it hadn't affected her, but by stone-facing them, she'd proven it had.

"That's how you have contacts with the police department," Ryan said, drawing her from her thoughts.

"Yeah. And all other government agencies. As well as I've kept a lot of my contacts on the street."

"Good. We have concerns about Brendan Darnell and wonder what the artist Patrick James could have gotten himself caught up in." Ryan sipped his iced tea.

"Something that could be smuggled in a painting,"

Shandra added.

Jenny leaned forward, looking interested for the first time. "Smuggled in a painting?" Her brown eyes lit up. "Are you thinking jewels, secret papers?"

Ryan shrugged. "We don't know what it could be."

Shandra went on to explain the poor quality of painting the victim had asked Jenny's cousin to make sure ended up in the exhibition. "Either so someone could purchase it—"

"Stop right there. If the person wanted to purchase it, there would have been a less public way. Just buy it from the artist, wrap it up, and haul it home." Jenny glanced back and forth between them. "And what would that have to do with Brendan Darnell?"

She said the name as if it she couldn't get it off her tongue fast enough. Ryan was beginning to think there were many women who found the man repulsive. Not just Shandra.

"All we know is he offered the artist a scholarship and at first he accepted and then—"

This time Shandra interrupted Ryan. "Only Brendan says Patrick accepted and then declined his offer."

Ryan nodded, that was true. "Billie said Patrick declined it when she was there."

"But not that he had accepted," argued Shandra.

"I wonder how we can figure out if that's the truth?" He glanced at Jenny.

"Leave that to me. I happen to know his social secretary."

"His what? Social secretary, I've never heard of that," Shandra said.

"That's because it's a job description Darnell made

up for this particular person. She knows everything he's doing only because he likes to talk…"

She left it unsaid but Ryan knew exactly what the woman meant. Darnell's social secretary was his paid lover. The minute it dawned on Shandra, she shivered.

"You have my number. Stay in touch and let me know what you dig up." Ryan picked up his drink.

"You do know the police are looking into this homicide." Jenny stood.

"But they are only looking as far as your cousin," Shandra said. "And I'm sure the only reason she didn't call for help was because she was in shock. They are making it out that she didn't call because she wanted to make sure Patrick was dead first."

Jenny shook her head. "Leilani could never hurt anyone intentionally. She has too soft a heart. Anyone that spends any time with her would know that. I'll keep you updated on what I find."

When the door closed behind the woman, Ryan turned to Shandra. "How did you know that was Leilani's cousin when we walked in?"

She smiled. "Same cheek bones, jaw line, and mouth. They had to be related."

He shook his head. He should have known his detail-oriented, artistic wife would notice something like that.

"What next?" Shandra asked.

"Jenny never told us what could be smuggled off the island in a painting. Let's go dig in the newspaper archives and see what the island has that someone else would want illegally."

Chapter Nine

The humidity and heat moistened her skin, Shandra found her energy seeping out with the perspiration. They'd found little that sounded as if it could be smuggled from the island for any money. Most of Kaua'i's most treasured things were places on the island. Alekoko Fish Pond, Wailiua Falls, and Ka Ulu o Laka heiau.

Ryan pulled his phone out of the leather holster on his belt. "It's Jenny."

Shandra nodded and slipped into the rental car as Ryan answered the phone. She stared at the rock walls and wide white overhang on the newspaper building. The Garden Island was written across the overhang. The nickname for the island was fitting. The greens of the trees, bushes, and grasses were stunning. The bright reds, yellows, whites, pinks, and lavenders of the flowers that grew everywhere gave the island a happy, welcoming feel.

Ryan slid in behind the steering wheel. "Jenny has someone who is willing to talk to us." He started the car and pulled out of the parking space.

"About Brendan Darnell?" Just saying the name churned her stomach. Hearing how he manipulated artists brought back memories of the man who'd manipulated her in college.

"No, he has information on what might be on the missing painting." Ryan drove them out of Līhu'e and back toward Kōloa.

"Did she give you any hint as to what?" Shandra hadn't discovered any old paintings that could be painted over to smuggle off the island.

"Only that we'd enjoy talking to him."

~*~

Ryan drove into a dirt parking lot alongside a hut selling coconuts, fruit, fresh fish, and drinks. Shandra noticed an old Suzuki Samurai without a top next to the hut and an older Mustang convertible, with the top down, parked in front.

"This is where we're supposed to meet this person?" Shandra stared into the shaded interior of the hut.

"That Mustang is Jenny's vehicle." Ryan exited the rental.

Shandra followed, more curious than ever about the man they were going to meet.

"Welcome," said a sun bronzed man, wearing a colorful button-up shirt, shorts, and flipflops. His long gray hair hung over his shoulders that were two boney points holding up the shirt. His face was narrow and etched with lines of laughter and age. His dark eyes twinkled.

"Hello," Shandra shook hands with the man. He felt like an old friend already.

Ryan greeted the man.

Jenny introduced them. "Ryan and Shandra, I'd like you to meet one of the local historians, Samuel Ukemana."

"Everyone calls me Sam," he said in a soft, warm voice.

"Pleased to meet you Sam." Shandra pulled over one of the sugar cane stools and sat beside Jenny.

"Fresh coconut milk." Sam placed coconuts with holes drilled and straws sticking out on the counter in front of them.

"Thank you." Shandra took a sip and smiled. "This is delicious!"

"You can't beat the freshness of our fruit on the island." Sam smiled proudly.

"Jenny said, you knew something about what we're looking for?" Ryan asked.

Sam frowned at him. "You are on the islands, relax."

Ryan frowned.

Shandra laughed. She understood the ways of telling stories. Since reconnecting with her Nez Perce family, she had learned there is a significance in each story and how it is told.

"Does this story have anything to do with art?" she asked.

"It depends on what you call art," the man said and smiled, his eyes twinkling. "As Ireland has it's 'little people' so does Kaua'i. They are the Menehune. Unfortunately, as the Leprechauns of Ireland bring good luck, the Menehune bring bad luck. Or so the stories have been told of bad things happening to those who see the little ones."

"What does this have to do with the death of an artist and a missing painting?" Ryan asked.

Shandra studied her husband. He was usually patient when it came to her family members telling stories, and he believed in her grandmother coming to her in dreams. Right now, he was acting closed minded.

"Ryan, give him time to get to the real message of the story." She put a hand on her husband's arm.

Sam smiled at her. "Your wife understands the purpose of a story."

She returned the smile and he continued.

"It's said that the Menehune followed Captain Trevane to the cave where he buried his money. He spotted them and told them not to tell a soul. Because he could see them and talked to them, they stole his memory. He couldn't remember where he buried the money. His wife and children spent their lifetimes trying to find the riches. They never did. There have been rumors of a map having been found that would lead the owner to the buried treasure." Sam leveled his gaze on each of them. "It's said it has been authenticated to the time the captain buried the treasure, which today would be worth more as a collection than it's true value."

"You think the map was going to be smuggled off the island or into someone's hands in the painting?" Ryan said. "And if that's true, the person responsible for the murder could be anyone of a hundred collectors of Hawaiian history." Ryan stared at Sam. He doubted this story had anything to do with the murder. It didn't make sense. There were so many other ways to have the map get into the hands of the highest bidder. Hiding it in a painting was too much like a bad movie.

"You have to admit the story is interesting." Shandra said, smiling at the orator.

"Yes, it is interesting, but I doubt it has anything to do with our murder." Ryan glanced at Jenny. She had a noncommittal expression. "Would you have listened to this story when you were a police officer?"

Jenny shrugged. "Sometimes there is more in the truth of a story than what you hear."

He shot a glance at his wife, who was nodding. He should have known she would feel the same way. Ryan sighed. "We'll take this into consideration. Any other ideas as to what could have been on the painting that someone would've wanted?"

"Do you have a photo of the painting?" Sam asked.

"No." Ryan studied his wife. "But you did take photos of each piece when it was brought in for the jurying process. Remember?"

Shandra's face lit up. "That's right! I'll call Leilani and ask her where those photos are. They took the photos so they would have the ones that would be in the exhibit to use for promotion." She pulled out her phone and started typing.

Ryan sipped his coconut and enjoyed the view of the ocean beyond. This could have been a relaxing vacation if they hadn't been staying with the main suspect in a homicide.

"Leilani says the photos are on her camera. She's going to download them to her computer." Shandra picked up her coconut and drained it. "Thank you for the refreshing drink and the wonderful story."

"You're welcome. Come again while you are on

the island. I have many more stories." Sam refused the money Ryan held out to him.

"Thank you, we will." Shandra said. She turned to Jenny. "Are you coming to Leilani's with us?"

The P.I. shook her head. "I'm going to see what I can find out at the police station. There's been enough time some forensics should have come through."

Ryan nodded. "Let us know what you find. And we'll do the same."

"Will do." Jenny stayed at the hut, while Ryan and Shandra walked out to the rental vehicle.

"I liked him," Shandra said.

"He reminded you of your family, didn't he?" Ryan knew his wife well. She hadn't been to the reservation for a while. It was time she went for a visit.

"He did. I think it's wonderful the way the indigenous people of this island hold onto their language and their stories. Now I want to know more about the Menehune and the story of the money."

"I have to admit the Irish in me finds the Island 'little people' interesting." He grew up hearing all kinds of stories about the 'little people' from his Irish mother.

"I'll look them up on the computer when I get home. Do you really think there is a 'treasure' map floating around?" Her skepticism renewed his faith in her deductive abilities.

"There probably are a lot of fake treasure maps that have suckered people into giving up money to own one." Ryan turned down the street to Leilani's house.

"I hope the photo gives us a clue about why someone killed Patrick."

Chapter Ten

Leilani had not only downloaded the photo to her computer, she had it on her television screen and had printed out three copies of the photo.

"This is great. Thank you for thinking of putting it on the television screen," Shandra said, standing back and viewing the garish painting. The screen had the painting sized to one and a half times the original. The enlarged top strokes appeared as if they were made in anger. They were thick and applied with force. The handle of the brush scraped through the middle of the stroke.

"It's almost as if he didn't want to paint this," she said, thinking out loud. "The strokes are completely unlike the paintings I saw in his studio."

Leilani picked up a magnifying glass and studied the photo in her hand. "It's as if he started out painting with his usual strokes and then used the thicker strokes to cover it up."

Shandra stared at her friend. "That's it! Something is hidden under the thicker paint." She glanced at Ryan. "Is there a way to see through the last layer of paint on a photograph?"

"Not a photograph. If we had the painting, there is a good chance we could discover what is under the bold strokes," Leilani answered. "I've been reading about how they are using special equipment to learn more about past painters' procedures."

Shandra stared at the photo. "Why would someone your cousin suggested we talk with tell us about the Menehune and hidden money?"

Leilani shrugged. "Menehune is the name my ancestors gave to the people who were here when they arrived. They were smaller and more primitive. The stories came about that the Menehune are bad little people who bring bad luck to those who see them."

"What would that have to do with Patrick's death?" Shandra asked, still trying to figure it out.

"I don't know why they would think his death had anything to do with the 'little people'. He didn't believe in such things. He laughed at me when I told him I put a faery garden in my back yard." Leilani stared at the television screen.

"Was Patrick interested in finding treasure?" Ryan asked.

The woman shook her head. "Not as in buried or shipwrecks. He was always trying to find easy ways to make money so he could paint more."

"Is that why he initially accepted Darnell's scholarship?" Ryan set the photo he'd been holding down on the coffee table.

Leilani nodded. "He only worked enough to

survive. He never turned down a meal if you invited him."

"Yet, he accepted the scholarship then turned it down later." Shandra studied her friend. "He must have found something that would sustain him for a while without the scholarship."

"I don't know what it was. We hadn't been that friendly the last month or so. If you want to know more about the last month, talk to Billie. She was his shadow for the last two months." There was a slight bit of jealousy snapping in her tone.

"Where can we find her?" Ryan asked.

"She has a small place up in Hanalei." Leilani wrote the directions on the back of one of the photographs.

"Thank you. Judging from the time, don't worry about us for dinner. We'll find something along the way." Shandra stood, picking up the photo.

Ryan led her out to the rental car. "For someone who says things were over with Patrick there was a barb of jealousy when she talked about Billie."

"I caught that too. Just because she might have been put aside for a younger woman doesn't mean she killed Patrick." Even though she knew murders had been committed for less, Shandra still didn't think her friend had killed the artist. She might have a broken heart, but she wouldn't take a life.

~*~

Hanalei was an hour and a half northeast from Kōloa. The miles weren't reflected in the time it took to drive them. Ryan sat in a line of cars waiting for it to move as they passed through Kapa'a. This town had many tourist type businesses. People crossed the street as they felt and cars slowed to peer into the shops.

"Do you think Billie will be home?" Shandra asked. "We should have asked for a phone number."

"Relax. Enjoy the views as we drive. If she's there great. If not, we'll find someplace to have dinner and then wait for her to return." Ryan grasped his wife's hand. "I know you want to clear your friend. But you also have to be prepared if she is arrested."

"What do you know that you aren't telling me?" she asked.

Ryan studied Shandra. "I'm just saying, your grandmother hasn't come to you in a dream. To me that means, you may be trying to save the wrong person." His belief in her dreams had helped her to believe in them.

"You are skeptical of the Menehune, but you are using the fact Ella hasn't come into my dreams to mean my friend is guilty." Shandra pulled her hand out from under his. "I've barely slept since we learned about the murder. She'll come tonight."

The rest of the drive to Hanalei was quiet. Ryan hoped Shandra would be open-minded if Billie had incriminating evidence against Leilani.

They followed the highway through the town of Hanalei. He noted several restaurants as they drove through. A quarter mile the other side of town, the note said to turn left. The small dirt path was just wide enough for their car.

A small bungalow sat at the end of the narrow road. There wasn't a vehicle present.

"It looks like she's not here," Ryan said, putting the car in reverse.

"Let's see. Maybe she doesn't have a car." Shandra

opened the door and stepped out.

Ryan put the car in park and followed his wife up to the door.

Shandra knocked. There was a soft sound of music playing. "Do you think she saw us coming and went out the back?"

Ryan wasn't sure what to think. "I'll go around back. You stay here." He stared in her eyes. "I mean it. Stay right here, on this side of the door."

She nodded.

He moved to the side of the house and walked to the back. There was a screen door. The inside door was open. He peered inside and found Shandra standing inside the house. He opened the screen door and strode through the small building to his wife. "I told you to stay outside."

She smiled. "You told me to stay on this side of the door. I am." She motioned to the front of the door.

"You know what I meant." He spun back to the interior of the house. Either the young woman was a slob or someone had been here tossing the place. "Don't touch anything. I'll check the other rooms."

Shandra didn't like the look of the displaced items. This wasn't a messy person. Someone was looking for something. Something small. Drawers were pulled out, books pulled off shelves, cushions out of chairs. This didn't make sense. The painting was missing. Why were they looking for something small? She hoped Billie was okay.

"The bedroom and bathroom are empty. But look as messy as this one." Ryan stood at the door between the open main room and kitchen.

"Do you think whoever did this has Billie?" she

asked.

"I don't know, but I'm calling Detective Kane." Ryan pulled his phone out.

"I didn't know you had his number." Shandra walked to the center of the bungalow and did a slow circle taking it all in as Ryan talked to the detective.

"He'll be here in a couple hours." Ryan walked to the kitchen, and using a towel, closed the door. "Come on. Let's grab something to eat and come back when Kane is here."

"You don't think Billie will come back and straighten things up?" Shandra wanted to stay and see if the woman returned.

Ryan took photos of the mess with his phone. "We'll have this evidence to question her about if she does come back and hides the fact her place has been searched."

It was hard to argue with that logic. Shandra walked out to the car as Ryan closed the door.

"Where do you plan to eat?"

Ryan grinned. "I saw just the place to take your mind off this."

She didn't have long to wonder what Ryan thought would make her forget a man was killed and a woman could possibly be missing.

He parked in a cobblestone and grass parking lot. They crossed the busy street to the side where businesses lined the sidewalk. Aromas of grilled pineapple, meat, and flowers filled her nostrils. Her stomach growled.

People milled about on both sides of the streets, entering and leaving the businesses.

Ryan walked up to the Kalypso Bar and Grill. It

was like a large Tahitian hut. The walls were only four feet high with open air seating. The place was packed.

"Aloha. Seating for two?" the hostess asked.

"Please. Any chance we can be along the side?" Ryan asked.

"We have one table open. Come this way."

They followed the young woman, dressed in shorts and a t-shirt, to a small table tucked in a corner of a small bamboo porch overlooking the street.

The sound of serving and conversations almost drowned out the calypso music.

A young man wearing board shorts and a t-shirt arrived to take their orders.

Shandra enjoyed watching the people on the sidewalks. They were all ages, all cultures, and all very happy. The breeze flowing through the open porch was welcome as the sun lowered and added its rays to the mugginess she felt.

When their meals were delivered, Shandra asked, "What do you think someone was looking for?"

Ryan studied her a minute. "What do you think?"

"The painting would be my guess but they opened drawers."

"Maybe that was to make the police think it was a small item." Ryan said logically.

"If Billie had the painting, she was at Patrick's studio the night he died. She could know who did it."

"Or she could have been the one who killed him." Ryan continued to study her.

Shandra thought about the small woman who had championed Patrick. She'd adored the man. Physically and emotionally, she didn't see the woman having what it would take to kill him. "I don't think so. I do think she could have seen something. Which worries me. Could the person who took the painting have taken her, too?"

Ryan grasped her hand. "This could be a crime of passion. Either of the women you are adamant didn't do it, could have pushed him over the cliff."

"That, I could believe might have happened in a moment of anger, but neither one of them would have finished him off." This she was certain of. Yes, a shove in anger, a misstep by Patrick. But not the cold-bloodedness of making sure he was dead. Which worried her that Leilani could have pushed him and her conscience made her try to go down the cliff to help him. But when she couldn't reach him, she'd been shocked at what she'd done and that was why she'd not thought clearly enough to call.

"Anyone is capable of anything given the right circumstances. You of all people should know that by now." Ryan picked up his iced tea.

She nodded. They'd solved enough murders together to know it wasn't always the logical person who killed. Some of the people who turned out to be the killers had surprised her. She sighed. "I know. But I still want to live with the hope that I can judge a person. I can't live my life skeptical of everyone like you do. You do that enough for the both of us."

Chapter Eleven

Detective Kane was getting out of his vehicle when
they pulled up to Billie's bungalow. Ryan put a hand on
Shandra's arm. "Stay here until I see what kind of a
mood he's in."

"Like whether or not he'll let us see the place
again?" She raised an eyebrow.

"Exactly." Ryan stepped out of the rental car and
walked up to the man watching him at the front door.
"It isn't locked."

The big man scowled. "How do you know it's
unlocked?"

"At least I didn't lock it when we called you."
Ryan tried to look contrite. It was hard to do, knowing a
crime had been committed behind the door the detective
was being belligerent about opening.

"When Shandra and I arrived, we knocked. We
could hear music playing. Listen you can still hear it.
It's a radio. I went around to the back. The door was

open. I went in and discovered the place had been tossed. I called you, and we went to Hanalei for dinner."

"You didn't touch anything inside?" The detective pulled a latex glove out of his pocket and used it like a rag to grip the door knob.

"Only the two doors, but I used a towel to close them."

The detective opened the door. The place looked as it had the first time he saw it. "It appears Billie hasn't returned," he said, hoping she was free to come back.

Kane whistled. "This place has been tossed. Why did you come here to see Billie?"

Ryan relayed what they'd learned from Leilani about Billie having been the deceased's shadow for the last two months. "We thought she might have an idea what the victim had done to make money since he'd turned down Darnell's scholarship."

The detective stopped taking photos and faced him. "Why do you think that is important?"

"Because there had to be something about the painting that he put in the exhibition that he wanted on display. We have photos of it and according to Shandra and Leilani, it appears he may have made the ugly, angry strokes on the top to hide something underneath. But we won't know unless we find the painting."

"That's all speculation. I've still got my money on the Brown woman."

"Then you're betting on the wrong pony," Shandra said from behind them.

Ryan and the detective spun around at the same time.

"What are you doing in this crime scene?" Kane

asked, clearly upset she'd entered the bungalow.

"I came to see if you had come up with any better explanation for this, and if you're going to put out an all points for Billie?" Shandra stepped up beside her husband, keeping her gaze on the detective.

"Why should I put an all points out on the woman who lives here?"

"It's obvious someone was looking for the painting and thought she had it. If that's the case, she's in danger." Shandra wasn't going to let the man's size or his glare keep her from saying her piece.

"Why is it obvious this place was tossed looking for the painting?" Detective Kane crossed his arms and studied her.

Shandra explained her reasoning and went so far as to tell him he needed to concentrate on Patrick's finances rather than Leilani.

She had to give him credit, he listened. Then turned to Ryan. "I'm not taking orders from you or your wife. I'll file this just like any other breaking and entering. As for the woman who lives here. We'll keep an eye out, but one murder on the island is unusual, I doubt there is going to be two." He waved them out of the bungalow.

Shandra was getting ready to dig in her heels, when Ryan took her by the arm. "Come on," he said in her ear.

She let him escort her out to the rental. "Now what?"

"Call Leilani. Don't tell her what we found, only that Billie wasn't here. Ask for a phone number and see if she knows of any friends Billie might be with."

Shandra dialed her friend.

"Hello?"

"It's Shandra. Billie wasn't home before dinner or after. Do you have her phone number?"

"It would be on the entry forms for the exhibition. I'll have to look through those." Footsteps and the sound of paper shuffling meant she'd gone into her office.

"Do you have any idea what friends she might be hanging out with?" Shandra wondered how much the artists on the island knew about one another. It was obvious they all had known Patrick well.

"She hung out mostly with Patrick but I think she and Elijah were friends, too. And Saul. Though I'm not sure how much they were friends or he used her knowledge of proportion to help him with his art." There was a pause. "Here it is." She rattled off Billie's number. "Do you think she knows something about Patrick's death?"

"We won't know until we can talk to her. Thanks." Shandra hung up and quickly tapped the number into her phone.

It rang and rang. "Hello?"

Shandra held her hand over the phone. "Detective Kane answered."

"Hang up. That means the phone is in the house. Which means she either ran from whoever came or someone has her."

She hit the end button. "Shouldn't we tell Detective Kane?"

Ryan shook his head and headed back toward Hanalei. "He'll figure it out because no one her age leaves a phone behind unless there's a reason."

~*~

An hour later, Shandra stared at the large home and beautiful yard of the residence they'd found for painter Elijah Lee. It sat atop a cliff, facing the ocean. The wind was just enough to dry the sweat on her skin, and cool.

"This is some place for a struggling artist to live," Ryan said, leading the way up the walkway to the impressive front door. He used the door knocker that resembled the head of a whale.

"No one said he came from money," Shandra said, watching the waves on the other side of the immaculate yard and rows of red and yellow flowering hibiscus. A flock of two colorful roosters and three hens scrambled into view around the side of a Mindanao gum tree. The colorful tree looked as if someone had splashed bright green, magenta, and blue paint at the top and smeared it down the trunk.

The door opened. "Hello? Oh my, Shandra, what are you doing here?" Mrs. Kim, one of the art society's board members, asked.

"We're looking for Elijah. This was the address we were given for him," Shandra replied, sharing a gaze with her husband.

"Oh, yes, he does live here. Well, in the back, in the pool cottage. Brendan isn't the only one in the art society who helps out young artists." She opened the door wider. "You might as well come through the house as go around. Then you'll be in cool air for a short time."

Shandra and Ryan entered the large open foyer. Paintings and sculptures filled the walls and open spaces on the floor where furniture wasn't needed.

"Elijah has been living in my cottage for nearly a

year now. He has put out some spectacular paintings." She stopped and pointed. "That's one."

The large five by five painting captured her attention. The scene was of a wet cave. A cave where the ocean can enter when the tide is up. Every vertical foot was a scene of the cave as the tide rose. The detail in the creatures and the sand in each time frame was spectacular. The small crab, crawling along the sand then picked up by the water and tumbled further into the cave.

"This is fantastic! The pride you must have knowing you have allowed this artist to concentrate on his craft." Shandra stood spellbound, taking in every nuance in the painting.

"I spend hours sitting in the chair over there studying this piece. Each time I find something new I didn't see before." She tapped Shandra's arm. "I paid a lot for this painting, but I know it would go for four times that if any other art lover ever sees it."

Shandra had to agree with the woman's statement. It was worth thousands.

"Come on. Elijah should be stopping soon for dinner. He usually eats about eight or nine and then paints until one in the morning. He doesn't get up until noon most days." Mrs. Kim took them out a double door onto a patio that overlooked an inground pool. The tropical plants in pots around the pool area and the small waterfall feature made the backyard look like a tropical oasis.

A small cottage sat beyond the pool and up against a forest of sandalwood and koa trees. Rock music blared from the open door and windows, drowning out the ocean beyond and birds in the trees.

"He likes to listen to music when he paints, which makes living back here a good place for him. Imagine if he were in town in a house or apartment?" Mrs. Kim motioned for them to continue. "I can't stand that racket."

"Does he play this all the time when he's painting?" Shandra asked.

"Yes. That's how I know the hours he paints." Mrs. Kim headed back the way they'd come.

"Just a moment." Ryan jogged after the woman. They talked and he strode back to Shandra.

"What did you ask her?"

"If Elijah was painting the night of the murder." Ryan motioned for her to enter the mouth of the blaring bungalow.

Shandra didn't budge. "What did she say?"

"He wasn't painting. She figured he was with his friends celebrating making it into the exhibition event though she knew he would."

Shandra added Elijah to the list of suspects until he could tell them where he'd been. With this information, she strode into the belly of the rock-n-roll beast.

The young artist was bobbing to the beat of the music as his steady hand put a delicate touch of color on a marine animal.

The music stopped. Shandra glanced around and saw the reason. Ryan had pulled the plug on a top of the line 80s stereo.

"Hey!" Elijah spun from his canvas. The anger etched on his face vanished when his gaze landed on her. "Ms. Higheagle, what are you doing here?"

"We," she motioned to Ryan, "were wondering if you knew where Billie is?"

"Billie? No. I haven't seen her since the night at the gallery. I bet she's broken up over Patrick. Those two were close." He put the paint palette down and dropped his brush in a jar of liquid. Wiping his hands on a towel hanging from a beltloop, he walked to a small refrigerator. "Want something cold?"

"What do you have?" she asked, watching Ryan prowl around the studio.

"Name your juice and I have it. Or there's beer and wine, if you want."

"Do you have guava?" She picked up a half dozen catalogs of art supplies off the one padded chair and placed them on a stack on the round block of wood used for a table.

"And you, Mr. Higheagle?" Elijah asked.

"It's Detective Greer. I'll have what Shandra's having." Ryan sat on the wood block table and catalogs.

Shandra held back a chuckle as the young man stared at Ryan.

"I'm sorry. I didn't. I mean…"

"It's okay, Elijah. You two were never formally introduced," Shandra said, giving her husband an admonishing look. He'd thrown the detective title out there to see if it shook the young man. She thought he'd passed that fine.

The artist handed them each a bottle of pink guava juice and dumped newspapers off a stool and sat in front of them. "Why are you looking for Billie? Something wrong with her ceramics at the exhibit?"

Chapter Twelve

Ryan wasn't falling for this young man's innocent
act. He knew Ryan's name. He'd told Elijah at the
event the other night when they were talking. And now,
asking about Billie. He knew something. What he
wasn't sure.

"No. Her ceramics are fine," Shandra said. "We
just wanted to talk to her. You know, because she and
Patrick were so close."

The artist bobbed his head. "She followed him
around like a lovestruck puppy dog."

"Did you see them together often?" Ryan asked.

"If there was a showing or art event she was
standing beside or behind him. She'd wait on him like a
damn slave." He glanced at Shandra. "Sorry."

Either the young man was raised right or he was
sucking up to Shandra, Ryan wasn't sure which.

"Did Patrick like Billie hanging around?" Shandra
asked.

The young man laughed. "When she wasn't around, he'd make remarks about her simpering and how she'd do anything he wanted." He peered into Ryan's eyes. "If you know what I mean."

This was different than what the women had said about Billie and the victim.

"We've been led to believe he could have any woman he wanted. Did he take advantage of Billie?" Shandra asked, her disgust barely hidden.

Ryan was sure the artist didn't hear it but knowing the woman, he did.

"Patrick liked to brag he could have any woman he wanted. And while he didn't give names, the rest of us had a pretty good idea he was playing with fire taking women to bed to get what he wanted."

"Sex?" Ryan asked.

Elijah shook his head. "No. He could get that anywhere. He didn't need to screw the old women for that." He glanced at Shandra again. "Sorry. I was brought up not to talk like that around women."

"That's good to know. I hope you don't treat women like Patrick apparently did." Shandra studied him.

The young man squirmed under her scrutiny. "I have my pride when it comes to taking someone to bed to get a favor."

"What kind of favors did Patrick get for bedding the 'older' women?" Ryan asked.

"Sometimes money. Art supplies. Food. It was how he survived while he painted, basically." He shook his head. "I wondered at his turning down Mr. Darnell's scholarship. It's not as good as what I have here with Mrs. Kim, but it would be better than taking women to bed to survive."

"Were any of the women married?" Shandra asked.

Ryan had started to wonder that as well. It would be another angle for his death. It appeared Leilani had known of the other women. And it sounded as if they all were willing to share him to keep him living in their midst.

"I don't know all of the women he took to bed." Elijah finished off his pineapple juice and glanced over his shoulder at the painting he'd been working on. He wanted to get back to work.

"Did his bedding all of these women upset Billie?" Ryan asked.

The young man shrugged. "I don't know. Billie and I aren't that good of friends." His cheeks darkened.

"Then why were you the first person we were told was her friend?" Ryan wasn't going to let that lie go.

Elijah cleared his throat and stared at the rag as he wiped his hands. "I don't know."

"There had to be a reason, we were told you were a friend," Shandra said in the tone she used when consoling someone.

It worked. The young man looked up at her. "We went to a few events together. It's hard for me to hang out with people my age. They haven't become dedicated to anything like I am to my art."

"When was this?" Ryan asked.

"Up until about three months ago." Irritation singed the words.

"Right before she became Patrick's shadow." Ryan studied the young man. "Did he steal your girl from you?"

"No! We parted as friends."

"But you and Patrick?" Shandra asked.

"He didn't deserve her fawning all over him. I couldn't figure out what she saw in him. He's a second-rate painter and a third-rate human being." Elijah rose and walked over to the record player, plugged it back in, and as soon as the music blared, he went to the canvas on the easel.

Their conversation was over.

Ryan held out his hand to Shandra. They walked out of the blaring cottage, by the pool, and around the house. They climbed into the rental.

Leaving the Kim residence, driving along the ocean, Shandra finally voiced the thoughts bouncing around in her head from their visit with Elijah.

"He and Billie were lovers, and she threw him over for Patrick. He could have decided to rub it in about Patrick's painting not being good enough to make the exhibit and they fought." She glanced over at Ryan.

He tipped his chin down once as if he kind of agreed with her.

"I can tell you this, that young man lies. I introduced myself to him the night of the event. He asked what I did and I told him I was a detective." Ryan flicked a glance at her then back at the road. "I'm not sure how much we can believe from him."

She stared out at the moonlight bouncing off the ocean.

"It's getting late. We'll have to visit with Saul tomorrow. It's time to go back to Leilani's and call it a night," Shandra said, hoping that waiting until tomorrow didn't give whoever ransacked Billie's bungalow either a chance to ditch her body or find her if she was hiding.

~*~

Leilani had gone to bed by the time they arrived at her house. She'd given Shandra a key to the front door since the murder, knowing the couple would be coming and going at all times as they helped prove her innocent.

"Today only added more people as suspects," Shandra said as they prepared for bed. "And Detective Kane only has one in his sights." She hated that the policeman was only trying to find evidence against her friend and not looking at all the other possibilities.

"He has more than Leilani. He was listening to us even if he sounded like he wasn't." Ryan kissed her and turned out the light.

"How do you know he was listening to us?" She lay on her back, staring up at the ceiling fan spinning in the slant of light from a streetlight and listening to the noises outside their open window beyond the whir of the fan.

"Because I know the look. Go to sleep. It's going to be a long day tomorrow with the reception tomorrow night." Ryan rolled to his side.

Ugh! She'd forgotten about the reception in her quest to prove her friend innocent. Being honest with herself, she didn't want to go to the reception. What if everyone thought her actions were what caused Patrick's death? She stared at the fan, spinning, spinning, spinning.

Sand ground between her toes and the warmth enveloped her feet. Shandra opened her eyes. She stood on a beach. It was more spectacular than any she'd walked on. The blue water of the ocean roared toward the shore. Waves burst up over rocks thirty yards off the beach. She searched the stretch of beach for Ryan but couldn't find him.

Grandmother sat on the rock, the waves crashing around her.

"Ella, get down, you'll wash away!" Shandra shouted and ran toward the rock. Water rushed up her legs. It wasn't cold, but warm and refreshing.

Grandmother held up a hand, stopping her from entering the water any further. Her other hand pointed toward the cliff.

Shandra's gaze followed the pointing finger and she saw a cave under the cliff. The ocean poured into the cave and ran back out. "What is this?" Shandra asked and glanced back at the rocks. Ella was gone.

Walking out of the water, Shandra strode toward the cave. The call of a seagull drew her gaze upwards. She frowned. Why did this cliff look familiar?

Crowing startled her awake. The pesky feral chickens roaming the island believed in heralding in each day at the crack of dawn.

Thin slices of sunlight painted lines on the wall opposite the window.

Friday was here.

Chapter Thirteen

Showering first, Shandra was dressed and waiting for Ryan when he walked out of the bathroom. "Ella came to me last night."

Ryan studied her and sat on the bed beside her. "What did you see?"

"A beach with a cave and a familiar cliff." She frowned. She still didn't understand the familiarity of the cliff. She didn't remember looking up at any cliffs since they'd arrived.

"Was there a sign to tell you which beach?" Ryan stood back up, drying and dressing.

She closed her eyes, remembering all she could. "No. There were rocks out in the water. Ella sat on them. The cave was to the, I want to say north of them, why I know that is the direction I'm not sure." That was what was so strange about the dreams Grandmother gave her. She knew things that she shouldn't.

"What about the cliff? What did it look like?" Ryan

was dressed and standing in front of her. She had his full attention.

"It was rock above the cave, all the way to the top. But the south side, where I was standing, it ran back, kind of like this…" She drew a stubby backward S. "On the side, lots of brush. There weren't any trees." She closed her eyes again, envisioning the cliff. "There was a rope dangling from the side."

Ryan grasped her hands, pulling her to her feet. "Let's get breakfast and search out Saul. Then we'll see if Jenny can help us find this cliff."

"That's a good idea. She should know someone who knows this island inside and out."

~*~

They'd been driving for forty minutes when Shandra asked, "Do you know where Saul lives?" She hoped they found Billie there and the woman was unharmed.

"In Hanalei."

"Really? Close enough Billie could have taken refuge there?" Shandra wondered if the woman had fled her bungalow when the person looking for the painting arrived.

"Do you know what I find interesting about the victim and Billie?" Ryan asked.

Shandra studied him. "What?"

"Patrick used women, and Billie seems to have all male friends."

Shandra couldn't think of any rebuttal to that. The two were an odd pair of friends in her estimation. Patrick had been open with the women about his need for their help and what he would give in return. But Billie…she never would have pictured the shy, hesitant

woman she'd seen as someone who used men.
However, it was obvious Ryan had picked up on it.

They continued through Hanalei following the
highway past the turnoff to Billie's.

"That's where Saul lives." Ryan pointed to a house
on poles to their right. The ocean peeked through the
trees and brush beyond the house.

"It's only a mile from Billie." Shandra wondered
why Ryan drove on by.

He parked the car in a wide dirt spot alongside the
road fifty feet beyond the driveway. An expanse of sand
and the ocean looked like a public beach.

"Why didn't you drive up to the house?" Shandra
scanned the windows of the house that could be seen
from this direction. Two. Tall trees shaded the house,
giving the artist little natural light to work with. The
yard was either bare or covered with tangled
underbrush. Three hens and a rooster scratched and
pecked at the bare earth.

"I thought we might come at them from the beach
side. More likely to catch them off guard." Ryan
twisted to the back seat and straightened, holding the
bag they'd prepared for beach excursions.

"You want to make it look like we just happened
upon them?" She doubted they would believe that, but
was willing to give it a try.

"We might get more out of them if we bump into
them casually than walk up to the door, knock and start
asking questions."

Shandra slipped out of her athletic shoes and into
her flipflops. "Let's go."

They walked up the beach, staying inside the trees,
then popped out onto the beach and walked back the

way they'd come.

As they drew closer to Saul's house, Shandra noticed there was someone outside in a hammock. The person appeared to be sleeping, with a hat over their face. "Do you see that?"

"Yeah. But look ahead."

Saul was jogging down the beach toward them.

Ryan pulled her closer and nibbled on her ear. He was just trying to make it appear as if they were enjoying the beach and one another. But it still made her heart race.

"Hey! What are you two doing up here?" Saul called as he jogged over to them.

"Just enjoying the beach. We don't have many days left here," Shandra raise her hand to shade her eyes and study him. "What are you doing here? Do you jog here every day?" He had a lean runner's body.

He stopped in front of them and pointed to the house. "I live here."

She twisted and studied the building. "I've never seen a house on stilts. Have you had the water come that high?"

"A time or two, it's been pretty high. Beats having to pump out a basement or first floor." He glanced at the house and back at them. "Would you like to come take a look at some of my projects?" he asked in a tone that sounded more like a little boy trying to garner acceptance.

She glanced at Ryan. "Do we have time?"

"We don't have anything to do until you get ready for the reception tonight." Ryan grasped her hand and they followed Saul to his house.

In the yard, the artist walked over to the hammock.

"Billie, wake up, we have company."

She didn't move.

"Come on. I know you don't sleep that hard." Saul bumped the hammock and the body flipped out onto the ground. He jumped back. "Stop…." His voice trailed off.

The knife sticking out of her back revealed how she'd died.

"Stand back," Ryan said, pulling his phone off his belt and dialing.

Shandra stepped up to Saul. "When did you last talk to her?"

"Before I went for a jog. She slept on the couch last night and said it was uncomfortable, she was going to catch some more sleep out here in the hammock." He turned away from the sight.

"Were you close?" Shandra followed the artist as he walked twenty feet away, toward the house.

"Don't go anywhere!" Ryan called to them.

Shandra put a hand on the man's arm. "You have to stay here. You're a witness to finding the body."

"Body?" He glanced over his shoulder and shuddered. "Why Billie?"

This was the most vulnerable the man had been since she'd met him. He'd had feelings for the woman.

"Ryan and Detective Kane will find out." She walked him over to a couple of beach chairs leaning against a tree. She opened one and motioned for him to sit as she opened the other and sat.

"What do you know about Billie and Patrick's relationship?" she asked.

His head bobbed up from where he'd been staring at his hands on his knees.

"You think they were both killed for the same reason?"

Shandra shrugged. "They are both artists. According to people we've talked to, they were seen together a lot the last couple of months…" She left that dangling.

"She and Elijah had something going on. I didn't understand when she started hanging out with Patrick. Elijah, yeah. He has talent and she could ride on his coattails. But Patrick! He was a passable painter. Could have sold paintings at bazaars and street corners but he'd never get a showing at a gallery." Saul looked her in the eye. He hadn't thought the dead man had talent. He'd said as much at the event on Wednesday.

Ryan joined them. "Detective Kane is sending a forensic team. He'll be along later." He turned over a bucket and took a seat. "Why was Billie here, sleeping in your hammock?"

Saul shook his head. "She showed up yesterday afternoon. Said someone had been hanging around her place and it scared her."

"Did she have anything with her when she arrived?" Ryan could tell by his wife's furrowed brow, she'd been in the middle of asking questions that had nothing to do with his line of inquiry.

"No. Just the clothes she had on. I tried to tell her to call the cops and she said it was probably someone harmless and she didn't want to get them in trouble." He chuckled. "She never wants—wanted to put anyone out."

"Why was she sleeping out here in the hammock?" Ryan asked.

"I told Shandra because she didn't sleep well last night." Saul stared down at his feet. "I shouldn't have gone jogging. But it helps me clear my head in the morning and get ready for work."

"Do you jog every morning?" Shandra asked.

"Yeah."

"How long are you gone?" Ryan knew why his wife had asked the question. It would set up that someone who knew his routine had used that to their advantage.

"Usually an hour."

"This morning?" Ryan had a feeling this morning had been no different. As much as he didn't care for the guy, he had been genuinely surprised when the body hit the ground.

"A little longer." His cheeks reddened. "There was a *wahine* that caught my eye. I visited with her." He rubbed a hand over his face. "Asked her to come to the reception with me tonight."

"You weren't bringing Billie?" Shandra asked.

He stared at her. "Why? We aren't-weren't a couple. Just friends."

"Did Billie call anyone after she came here?" Ryan drew the man's attention back to him.

"Not that I know of. She didn't have her cell phone and didn't ask to borrow mine."

"Did you tell anyone she was here?" They had to establish how the killer knew to find her here. Ryan was pretty sure this hadn't been a random act. She was connected to the victim from Wednesday night.

Sirens pierced the air. Ryan rose. "Would you show the police back here please?"

Saul nodded and headed to the front of his property.

"What did you learn?" Ryan asked Shandra as the

man disappeared around the side of the house.

"Saul doesn't understand her infatuation with Patrick, and she arrived here saying someone was hanging around her place making her nervous." Shandra stared at the body. "What did you learn?"

"Not much. It looks like a rare knife or a replica of one."

"Did you get a photo?" Shandra interrupted.

Ryan grinned. "Yes. We'll add it to our things to ask Jenny and her associates about. It looked like one swift stab. She was probably sleeping and whoever killed her walked up, thrust the knife up under the hammock, and walked away."

"Any footprints?"

"Not that I could tell."

The forensic team arrived.

Ryan motioned to the men and women carrying cases. "I'll take care of these guys. Make sure Saul doesn't slip away before Kane gets here."

Chapter Fourteen

It was closing in on noon when Ryan drove them to the coffee shop/deli to meet up with Jenny. Shandra wasn't sure if she could eat anything thinking about the two artists that were now dead.

Once they walked through the door, the scent of cinnamon and cheeses started her mouth watering. "This was a good choice," she told Ryan.

He grinned. "I thought you would approve."

Jenny sat at a table in the corner.

They ordered and sat with her.

"What have you learned?" Ryan asked.

"Brendan Darnell has been living large on his family's money and his bank accounts are dwindling." Jenny shoved several papers across the table. "According to my source who gave me these copies, Darnell is the one who took back the offer of the scholarship when he realized he needed to start pinching pennies."

"Interesting. So Patrick did have to look somewhere else for money while he painted." Shandra studied the papers. Seeing the items the man spent money on, her stomach churned. She shoved the papers all over to Ryan.

"Did you hear Billie Moon is dead?" she asked Jenny.

The P.I. nodded. "I was over at the P.D. when the call came in." She nodded to the papers. "I've had Darnell watched. He couldn't have killed Billie. According to my contact, he was 'busy' when the other one went over the cliff."

Shandra didn't want to think about what she meant by 'busy.' "He's a scuzz ball but not a killer."

A high school aged girl delivered their lunch. She smiled at them and exchanged pleasantries with Jenny, while Shandra looked through her sandwich to make sure onions hadn't landed anywhere in her meal.

"Do you know everyone on the island?" Shandra asked, before taking a bite of her ham and swiss with fresh pineapple slices.

"It's a small island. Many of us are related, even if in a small way." Jenny shrugged and sipped her iced tea. "You were saying something about finding a cliff." The P.I. turned her attention to Ryan.

Shandra felt a knot in her stomach. How did they explain to the woman that she'd seen the cliff in a dream and they wanted to find it? Sure, Jenny had seemed to believe in the Menehune like their orator Sam, but this was personal to Shandra.

Ryan glanced at her, took her hand, and then leaned over the table and spoke in a quiet voice. "This is going to sound odd. But since you believe in the

Menehune, I'm hoping you will believe what I'm going to tell you."

Shandra sat still, watching the woman's blank face as Ryan told Jenny about her dreams, her grandmother, and her heritage. He ended with. "Last night Shandra's grandmother showed her a cliff. We don't know what it means, but usually it has something to do with a murder I, we, are working on."

Jenny shifted that unemotional face Shandra's direction and a huge smile broke out. "That's why you understood Sam's storytelling and believed in the Menehune."

"Please don't tell anyone. Especially Detective Kane. He doesn't like my being mixed up in the investigation," Shandra said, feeling as if the gravel that had been slowly mixing in her stomach had turned into ice and melted away.

"I would say, we need a helicopter to fly around the east side of the island. You say you felt the ocean was east?"

Shandra nodded. "And the cliff was west."

Jenny pulled out her phone and stood. "I'll make a call and see if my cousin's helicopter is available this afternoon." She walked away.

"I can't believe you told her about my dreams," Shandra said, facing her husband.

"After hearing the story from Sam and seeing how both he and Jenny liked seeing how you embraced their culture, I had a feeling she'd understand." Ryan picked up his sandwich. "Eat up so we're ready for this helicopter ride."

~*~

Two hours later, they lifted off the ground at

Hanapēpē. Ryan had been in a helicopter while in the military and as a detective with the Weippe County Sheriff Department. He held onto Shandra's clammy hand as they rose into the air.

Jenny and her cousin, Huko, sat in the cockpit. He and Shandra were in the back with headsets on.

"We're going to start down here and slowly move along the coast line," Jenny's voice rang through the headset.

"That's a good idea," Ryan said, into the microphone connected to the headset. He clicked the button that would only allow Shandra to hear him. "Are you doing okay?"

She nodded, but her wide eyes and pale face said otherwise.

"Take a deep breath and let it out slowly. Nothing's going to happen."

Jenny's voice interrupted. "Look out in the water. There's a pod of spinner dolphins."

Shandra leaned across him and peered out the window. "Oh! They are so graceful!" She grabbed Ryan's hand and squeezed. "Do you see them?"

"Yes." He gave the pod a brief glance. It was more fun watching the happiness on Shandra's face. Her color was back, and she was no longer worrying about being up in the air.

"Tell me more about this cliff," Huko said.

Shandra sat up and stared out her window at the coast line they followed. "It was rocky, with a wet cave at the bottom and a rock sticking up out of the ocean about fifty feet out. Water splashed up over the rock."

"I can think of three places along this side of the island that are possibilities. Mainly because of the cave." The helicopter moved a little faster. "I'll let you know when we are getting close to them."

Shandra nodded and leaned back in her seat, staring at the coastline.

Ryan held onto her hand. "We'll find it."

"I hope so."

~*~

Fifty minutes later Huko's voice sounded in Shandra's ear. "This is the first cliff we'll come to that has a wet cave near the base."

The helicopter flew in closer to the shore and hovered. Shandra studied the cave, the rock, and glanced up the cliffside. "This looks like it." She stared at the spot where she'd noticed what looked like a rope. "Can you go a bit closer to the south side of the cliff?"

The helicopter rose slightly and moved closer to the brush. The end of the rope dangling off a rock ledge moved. "There! See the rope! This is it. This is the cliff."

Jenny spun in her seat and looked at Shandra. "This is Halekoa Point."

"Where Patrick fell off the cliff," Ryan added.

Shandra sank back against the seat. Why had Grandmother shown her this cliff? They knew this was where the murder happened. But she'd shown her the cave first, then the rope hanging from the cliff.

"Can you land at the beach and let us look around?" she asked.

"I can land on top if the cops are gone. This beach is private." Huko raised the helicopter, and they peeked over the top. All that sat on the lonely point was Patrick's studio.

Huko set the helicopter down. They all removed

their headgear and stepped out of the aircraft once the blades had stopped.

"There has to be a reason that rope is dangling on the side of the cliff," Shandra said, heading to the spot where she'd seen the police showing interest.

"Hey, don't get to close to that edge until I've checked it out," Ryan said, taking hold of her hand, slowing her down.

"Where exactly did Patrick go over the edge?" she asked, knowing Ryan had been here the night it had happened.

"Up here where the ground is all trampled."

They stopped and stared down the cliffside. A shiver trembled through her. A man she barely knew, but who had been angry with her decision, had died here.

"Can we climb down?" she asked, studying the path that had been made by the forensic team.

"If you go slow." Ryan held her hand, keeping her from moving as he faced Jenny and Huko. "We're going to take a look. I'd appreciate it if you two kept an eye on us."

"I have some parachute cord in my copter," Huko said. "We could tie it around your waist. But there's only enough for one person." He shrugged.

"We'll be careful." Shandra stepped to the edge. "I need both hands to climb down this."

Ryan released her and followed.

The scent of the ocean rose on the wind curling up the side of the cliff. It mingled with the damp earth and sweet scent of plumeria. As she neared a flat surface that had flattened vegetation and a dark spot, she realized was blood, the scent she now knew as death, lingered.

"That's where they found him," Jenny called down.

Shandra wasn't sure how the woman knew, but she believed her.

"This way. The rope was hanging over this way," she said, leading Ryan to the side of the flat spot. "Do you think the police found the rope?"

"If Jenny says that was where the body was, she saw the report." He had his phone in his hand. He scrolled and hit a button. "Jenny, did the police report say if they found the rope?" He listened and Shandra peered over the edge of the cliff.

Ryan put the phone on his belt. "She said there was no mention of the rope. But they only went down the cliff about twenty feet and stopped. They believed all the evidence would have been from the body up the cliff."

"That rope was down a lot farther than twenty feet." Shandra glanced up and then down. "I think we should either tell Detective Kane or come back tomorrow with our own ropes and look for it."

"I agree. You have a reception to attend in three hours."

Chapter Fifteen

The makeshift gallery in the mall was lit up like a
showing at a prestigious art show. Ryan led Shandra in
and was surprised to see so many people. There was
barely space to walk as they made their way across the
room to where Leilani and Mrs. Kim stood.

"Shandra, Ryan, I was beginning to wonder if you
were going to make it," Leilani said, concern lacing
each word. She leaned closer. "We heard about Billie.
Did you talk to her before…"

Shandra shook her head and motioned to the
deceased woman's ceramics she'd picked for the event.
"I see you are celebrating her art."

Ryan glanced over and noticed the woman's
ceramics were nestled in a ring of leis. He wished
they'd had a chance to talk to her. Perhaps they could
have kept the killer from her and solved Patrick's death.
Now they had two homicides that were connected.
Even Detective Kane couldn't deny that fact.

While driving to the reception, Ryan had called Kane and told him about the rope that was hanging from the cliff where Patrick had died. The detective had acted unconcerned, saying it was probably from some kids goofing around at some point. Ryan didn't take it so lightly. Someone had to have access to the spot where the victim died. With so much activity up top, the logical direction for them to get away was down. But how had the rope happened to be there?

"Earth to Ryan," Shandra said, placing a glass of wine in his hand.

"Sorry. I was thinking about that rope."

"The one Detective Kane believes is of no consequence?" She sipped her wine.

"Yeah." His gaze landed on the newest arrivals. "Look who's here."

Shandra spun around. "Brendan and his 'social secretary?'"

"That would be my guess." He glanced down at his wife, the distaste in her eyes was hard to miss. "How about I keep Darnell busy and you visit with the secretary?"

Relief softened her previously taut facial features. "That sounds like a good idea. Anything specific you want to know?"

"Just the whereabouts of Darnell during both murders and if she has any idea what he is doing to keep money flowing in."

Shandra nodded. "I can do that."

They walked toward the couple together. He had to give Shandra credit, she plastered a smile on her face when Darnell acknowledged her.

Ryan started speaking to the man, making him face

away from his date. Shandra stepped over to the woman and led her away.

"Do you think all these deaths are going to hurt this event in coming years?" Ryan asked, starting with the innocent questions.

The man puffed up. "I can't believe that poor Billie is also gone. The two lovebirds. Did she take her own life?"

"Lovebirds? That's not what the artists are saying. Did you know something about the two being more than friends?" Ryan would believe the half dozen other art community members he'd spoken with over this blow hard. But he wondered at the man trying to push that theory.

"Oh, I happen to know she would go to his studio at all hours of the night. If that isn't a booty call, I don't know what is." His gaze roamed around the room until it landed on his 'secretary'. He started to take a step that direction.

Ryan put a hand on the man's chest to stop him. "You didn't answer my question about if this will influence what happens to this event in the future."

Darnell glared at him. "How the hell should I know? I'm not a psychic. Look at the crowd now. It's brought in more people. We usually only have half this many." He shoved by Ryan, headed for his arm candy.

~*~

Shandra smiled at Francie. They'd started out with pleasantries. Shandra mentioned she knew Jenny and they started chatting like old friends. She liked the young woman. What she really wanted to say, was get away from that man before he steals your youth and independence.

"I understand you can vouch for Brendan's whereabouts the night Patrick died?" Shandra sipped her wine and noticed the woman's gaze flicked toward the man and returned.

"Yes. But he didn't come home from the event right away. I don't know what time poor Patrick died, but Brendan didn't come home until well after midnight." She cringed. "If he heard me say that he'd be furious, but I do believe in telling the truth whatever anyone thinks about me."

"Thank you. The truth is all I want. What about this morning? About ten?" Shandra noticed Ryan putting a hand on the man's chest. She wouldn't have much more time with the woman.

"He always goes golfing early in the morning, when it's cooler. He wasn't home until about eleven-forty-five. He always comes home for meals unless he has a meeting where the food is supplied." She grinned. "He likes his food as much as he likes…" She didn't have to finish the sentence.

"What kind of meetings does he have? I thought he had family money he lived on."

"He did, but he's been using it up too fast. He's been having meetings with finance managers. He told me the other day, if he can't find a way to make money, he was going to have to kick me out, because he can't afford to keep me." She didn't sound heartbroken. "Honestly, I'm looking forward to the day."

"Why don't you just leave?" Shandra couldn't believe the woman would stay if she could walk away.

"I'm still putting feelers out for another opportunity. I don't want to be out on the street until I find something else."

"What are you two talking about?" Brendan asked, walking up behind Francie and putting his arm possessively around her waist.

"The event and life," Shandra said, pivoting and catching sight of Ryan. He was talking with Celia the other potter who had made the show. She walked over and caught the last of the question Ryan asked.

"…Billie and he lovers?"

Celia made a noise in her throat and chuckled. "No. Patrick wouldn't have slept with Billie, he knew she was Elijah's girl."

Shandra stepped up to them. "Elijah and Billie were in a relationship?" She scanned the crowd for the young painter. It dawned on Shandra she hadn't seen him since arriving. With his painting being the focal point of the exhibition with the highest prize ribbon, he should have been mingling and accepting congratulations as well as offers for his work.

"Where is Elijah?" she asked.

Celia shrugged. "I'm sure he was here when I arrived. He's probably surrounded by potential buyers and you can't see him."

Shandra pulled Ryan away from the potter. "Let's split up and see if we can find him. If they were in a relationship, he has to be broken hearted and maybe can shine some light on her death."

Ryan didn't budge. "Remember what he told us? He and Billie were just friends. But when we asked him specifically, his cheeks reddened. I could tell he was lying about something but I didn't know what."

"You think it was that he and Billie were in a relationship. But why did she start following Patrick around?" Shandra studied her husband. He had a good grasp of the criminal mind, but she thought he might be off on this one. "What about Grandmother showing me the cliff and the cave below? What could that have to do with Billie and Elijah?"

"I don't know." Ryan shook his head and put a hand on her lower back. "Let's go look for Elijah and ask him."

They wandered through the large room, visiting here and there and ended up in front of Elijah's painting. Mrs. Kim stood by the painting answering questions.

"Where's Elijah?" Shandra asked, when the last person moved on.

"Oh, he wasn't feeling well and left shortly after arriving. He looked awful. I think he's got the flu or something." The older woman looked concerned. "He would never miss this event otherwise. Especially when his painting won such acclaim!" The woman beamed as she gazed at the ribbon.

"Had you talked to Elijah any time before he arrived here?" Ryan asked.

"No. But about two his music stopped blaring." She shook her head. "Such a tragedy about Billie. Sweet child."

"We heard tonight that she and Elijah were in a relationship. Is that true?" Shandra asked.

The older woman's face softened. "He did his best work when she was around." She faced the painting hanging on the wall. "He painted this when she was still with him."

"Why did she leave?" Shandra asked in a soft voice.

"I'm not sure. And it wasn't like she left all

together. I saw her sneaking through the pool area many nights, headed for the studio. It was as if they didn't want anyone to know they were still together." She inhaled air and spun toward Shandra. "He's not sick, he has a broken heart!"

"Do you know when Elijah found out about Billie?" Ryan asked.

"No. But that has to be why he's sick. He must have heard it from someone when he arrived." The older woman started fussing. "I need to go home and console him. He mustn't do anything stupid."

"Like what?" Shandra asked, even though she could see by the fear on the woman's face, she was thinking he might take his own life.

"Ruin the paintings he made while she was alive or… heaven forbid. Try to join her." The woman hurried out the door, bumping several people in her haste.

"What were those two up to that they faked their relationship had ended and Billie became Patrick's shadow?" Ryan asked.

Shandra knew he was thinking out loud, but it was a huge question that might solve the murders.

Chapter Sixteen

Shandra woke having had the same dream as the night before. The cliff, cave, and rock. Only this time there was also a boat in the distance. They all had to be clues.

"We should go talk to Elijah this morning," Ryan said, dressing.

"After we go to the cliff." Shandra pulled on long pants and her hiking boots.

"We might learn what was going on by talking to Elijah," her husband persisted.

"But I had the same dream last night. Only this time there was a boat in the distance. It's important to check this out or else Ella wouldn't keep showing it in my dreams." She straightened from tying her boots and stared at Ryan. "If we have something concrete to question Elijah about, besides his and Billie's involvement, I think we'll get more out of him." She smiled. "And you said Detective Kane wasn't taking the cliff information seriously."

"Okay, it's not going to matter if we talk to Elijah this morning or this afternoon." Ryan kicked off his athletic shoes and put on his hiking boots. "We'll have to stop by an outdoor store and get some climbing rope."

"And breakfast. Leilani didn't come in until late last night. I don't want to disturb her by digging around in the kitchen." Shandra had wondered about her friend coming in well after midnight when the event only lasted until nine. But as Ryan had mentioned, she may have a social life they'd been cramping by staying with her.

"I noticed it was close to one when she came home. Do you think she's 'close' with all the male artists?"

Before Shandra could state he was making a conclusion from nothing, he added, "She came home late the night Patrick stormed out of the event and she came in late last night after Elijah was a no show."

"She is friends with all of the artists. She could have gone to make sure he was okay." She quickly added, "Which makes her sympathetic, not a killer."

Ryan shrugged and picked up a backpack he'd put together last night when they'd returned from the reception. "Let's go."

~*~

Jenny joined them at the cliff. She'd called to see when they planned to check it out while they were eating breakfast and Ryan had invited her along. His comment, "She's ex-police and still has connections. If we find something it would be good to have her corroborate and phone it in."

Shandra agreed. And she liked the woman. She

was all business but also knew how to have fun.

"I brought my climbing gear and I borrowed some from my brother. I have enough for all three of us," Jenny said, pulling a duffel bag out of the backseat of her car.

"I bought some rope but didn't get the full gear. Didn't want to buy it for a one-time thing," Ryan strode toward the other woman and her car.

Shandra faced the ocean. She stared out at the water, watching the waves, looking for a boat. Had the one in her dream been the exact boat, or was it just a metaphor for something else? Something bobbed in the waves to the far right. A surfer. The more she watched, half a dozen began popping up on boards and riding the waves toward shore.

Surfers weren't in her dream, and they wouldn't have been out at night when the murder happened.

"Come get into a harness," Ryan called. He and Jenny were already harnessed up and spraying bug repellent.

Shandra hurried over. Ryan helped her into a harness. They'd rock climbed several times for enjoyment. This would be her first time actually looking for evidence. She sprayed the bug repellent on herself and Ryan grabbed the two coiled ropes Jenny pulled out of the duffel bag.

"Jenny's going to go first, then you, and then me," Ryan said, as they walked to the edge where Patrick had gone over.

"What are we attaching the ropes to?" Shandra asked.

"There should be anchors from the forensic team and body retrieval," Jenny said, turning to face the cliff and going down backwards, using her hands to grab vegetation. "Here's one." The P.I. hooked her rope into an anchor and moved down the side of the cliff out of their way.

Shandra stepped over the edge and found another anchor about eight inches over and down from Jenny's. She spotted two others that Ryan could use to hook into.

The climb down to the first ledge where the body had fallen was easy. On down to the second wasn't hard either.

Once they dropped off that ledge, Jenny called out. "There's a bit of a trail over here. It's where the rope is dangling."

Shandra shifted over to the area. She heard clicking and presumed Jenny was taking photos before she and Ryan came through and messed up any evidence.

The brush scraped at her arms. Shandra was glad she'd thought to put on long pants and bug spray. The scent of the ocean grew as they lowered down the cliff.

"I'm running out of rope, what about you two?" Jenny called up.

"I am," Shandra said, noting the ten feet she had left.

"Me, too," Ryan said from above her.

"We'll have to go the rest of the way on foot." A couple of clicks and Jenny growled out what sounded like a curse word.

"You okay?" Shandra tried to look down but all she could see was brush and ferns.

"I'm okay. I missed the trail. Hang there until I find it." There was some grunting and the sound of brush cracking and swishing.

Ryan arrived beside Shandra. "You doing all right?" he asked.

She smiled. "Yes. This is fun other than I'm trying to figure out how someone would have known Patrick fell if they had been clear down here. The person had to have been up top, quarreled with him, and when he fell, followed to make sure he was dead. He wasn't. They finished him off and must have heard Leilani coming and came down this way."

"Can you see me? Try to get over here as close as you can," Jenny said.

"In which case, the person would have lots of healing scratches if they hadn't been prepared to make this trek." She pushed off the cliff, with branches snagging her pant legs and landed closer to where Jenny stood below her.

"Go to the end of your rope, click off, and then grab whatever you can to get down to me," Jenny said.

Shandra unhooked from the rope and used both hands to grasp a fern and a bush. She wished she had gloves. The killer would have wished the same thing if leaving this way had been unforeseen.

Ryan waited until Shandra was down next to Jenny before he swung over toward them and moved to the end of his rope. Whoever escaped this way, would have had to have knowledge of the trail and the rope. He'd caught a glimpse of the faint trail Jenny was following. While it wasn't a well-traveled path, it had been traveled enough to be easily seen.

He latched onto whatever he could find to keep his downward momentum from tumbling him into the women. When he was standing beside them, he motioned for Jenny to continue.

The trail was now on a gradual downhill at the base of the cliff. Every twenty feet the vegetation was low enough he could get a glimpse of the beach and ocean beyond.

They stepped out of the brush and set foot on the beach, close to the base of the cliff.

"Where would someone go from here?" he asked.

Jenny peered down the beach. "Either get picked up by a boat or walked the shoreline until they came to someone who could give them a ride."

"Is there access to this beach?" Shandra asked.

"Only by hiking in. There isn't a parking area close by." Jenny started along the cliff. "Let's take a look inside the cave."

"Is that safe?" Shandra asked.

"This time of day it is. The tide is out and shouldn't come back in until later."

Ryan made a note of what Jenny had said about access to this beach. He studied the rock sticking thirty feet out of the water and sand. Shandra said there was water all around the rock in her dream. That meant it had been high tide.

They approached the entrance of the cave. It was a good forty feet across and twenty feet high.

"How high do you think the water comes in here?" Shandra asked.

"See the marks on the side of the cave?" Jenny pointed to a salty white line about six feet up the wall.

"That's a lot of water." Shandra glanced back out the cave entrance to the ocean.

"We'll be fine," Ryan said, stepping beside her and putting an arm around her shoulders.

"A small boat could come into this cave and

remain unnoticed," she whispered.

She was thinking about the boat in her dream the night before.

Ryan gave her shoulders a squeeze. "A small boat could."

They walked as far back as they could using the light from the entrance. Ryan slid his backpack off his shoulders and pulled out a flashlight. "Let's see how much farther this goes." He shone the beam into the darkness and grasped Shandra's hand.

Chapter Seventeen

Shandra wasn't sure if it was the coolness in the cave or the eeriness of the dark enveloping them that caused the hair on her arms and neck to tingle. They'd walked a good forty feet more into the darkness of the cave.

Every few steps, Jenny would touch the back of Shandra as if she were just making sure she wasn't falling behind. Her touch and the grasp Ryan had on her hand, helped Shandra keep moving forward, knowing she wasn't alone.

A glint of something metal shone in the beam of the flashlight.

"What was that?" Shandra asked.

Ryan kept the beam on the box and walked up to it. "It looks like an old ammunition box. What would it be doing here?" He peered at Jenny who stood on the other side of Shandra.

"I'm pretty sure there wasn't anything stored on

this island during the war," Jenny said. "And those would be rustier if they'd been here that long. Not to mention, I'm pretty sure when high tide comes in this would be under water. See how wet it is now?"

"Then someone put this here, for what? To be hidden until the next tide or to be picked up?" Shandra stepped forward.

Ryan put a hand on her arm. "Jenny take some photos, then we'll open it."

Several flashes of her phone and Jenny walked forward. "It's locked."

"I can try to break the lock," Ryan offered.

"Just give me some light." Jenny dug into the small crossbody bag she had on and pulled out what looked like a lock picking kit.

Ryan held the light and Jenny deftly picked the lock.

Shandra had all kinds of thoughts running through her head. What would someone smuggle via this cave and the tides?

"Here you go." Jenny opened the lid.

Packages sealed in multiple plastic bags filled the box.

"What is it?" Shandra asked. It looked like crushed ice.

"Drugs. Specifically, meth," Ryan said.

Jenny clicked more photos and closed the lid. "We need to get this to HIDTA. It's the Hawaiian drug enforcement group."

"Let's go." Ryan took Shandra's hand.

They hurried out of the cave faster than they'd walked in. Now they knew what the cave was being used for. "How does this tie into Patrick and Billie's deaths?" Shandra asked.

"We don't know, but whoever killed Patrick knew how to navigate the cliff to this beach." Ryan stood at the entrance of the cave still holding Shandra's hand. This was more than a murder investigation now. He wanted to get Shandra back to Leilani's and sit down with Jenny to learn all he could about the trafficking of drugs on the island.

"Do you think Patrick was dealing drugs to help fund his art?" Shandra asked.

Ryan studied his wife. She'd been his rock through most of the murders they'd solved, but having the victims be artists she'd met and perhaps having dealt drugs, she was having trouble putting the two together.

"We don't know. Maybe he stumbled across the cave, explored, and discovered what we did. Maybe he waited, discovered who was picking up the box and then tried to blackmail them. Or maybe he wanted a cut. We may never know, but it could very well be what killed him." Ryan glanced at Jenny.

She was on her phone. Like a good ex-cop she was calling in what she'd found. He bet her superior wished she hadn't quit the department and that was probably why they gave her information so freely.

Shandra released his hand and walked to the edge of the water, staring at the rock.

Jenny finished her call and walked over. "The drug task force will put surveillance on this cave. They said there has been a new influx of drugs and they couldn't figure out where it had been coming from." She grinned. "We just found their source."

Ryan smiled. "Nothing like knowing you caught someone who's been flying under the radar."

"Yeah." She glanced around. "Let's get out of here. No telling who might come by for that box."

"The only way back to the vehicles is up." Ryan glanced up the cliff and sighed heavily. The up was going to be much worse than the down.

~*~

"Lunch is on me." Jenny said as they slipped out of their climbing harnesses at the top of the cliff.

Shandra studied the woman. Jenny looked as if she climbed two hundred feet cliffs covered in brush every day. Her arms ached from the scratches and the strain of hanging onto the rope. Her legs were a bit limp as well. But her stomach was growling. "Sounds good."

Ryan took her gear, putting it in the duffle bag with the ropes. "We'll follow you. Hopefully it's not too far away, I'm starving."

"Not too far." Jenny tossed the duffel bag in her car, slammed the door, and stared at the studio. "Did the victim own the studio?"

Shandra stared at the structure. She hadn't noticeed how out of place it looked up here before. A flat expanse of Halekoa Point waved with the tall slicing grass she'd learned was called Buffalo grass. There were half a dozen Kca trees strung out along the point, their powerful trunks bent to the onslaught of the wind. The studio, wasn't a quant bungalow, but rather a modern looking small version of a lighthouse. This far from the water and sitting with trees, it seemed out of place.

"I would think you could learn that from your contacts at the police department," Ryan said.

Shandra faced him. "We should find out if he had any next of kin to see what will happen to his paintings." Though she found herself thinking it a bit macabre, she was interested in owning one of Patrick's paintings. One where his talent showed. It would be a way for her to keep his memory alive.

"I can tell you he has parents and a sibling in North Dakota," Jenny said. "I think the parents are coming to get the body. I guess they'll figure out what to do with his paintings."

"I'll leave my name and phone number with Detective Kane. I'd like to speak to them." Shandra slid into the passenger side of the rental car.

Ryan lowered into the seat and closed the door. He shifted to face her. "Why do you want to see Patrick's family?"

"I would like one of his paintings."

"I see." Ryan centered himself behind the steering wheel and followed Jenny's vehicle. "Why would you want one of his paintings?"

She explained her thoughts on keeping his memory alive.

"What about Billie?" Ryan asked.

"I plan to purchase something of hers as well."

"You can't make a shrine to them." Ryan turned down a dirt road, following Jenny.

"I won't. I'll figure out an art museum to donate them to." Shandra held onto the door handle. "What kind of a road is this?"

"I don't know, but I'd sure like to know where she's taking us." Irritation rang in Ryan's voice.

"You've survived longer than this without a meal," Shandra chided him.

"It's not because I'm hungry. I don't like that we just found a drug stash and someone we barely know is taking us out into an unpopulated area."

Shandra didn't understand Ryan's distrust of Jenny. She'd been steering them in all the right places so far. "I guess we'll see where she's taking us and deal with it then."

They rounded a corner and a small cluster of huts sat tucked at the edge of what could only be described as jungle with a sandy beach stretching out before it and people frolicking at the water's edge.

"This looks very sinister," she joked as Ryan pulled their car up alongside Jenny's.

Small children ran out, singing, "Jenny. Jenny. Jenny."

Shandra exited the car before Ryan and walked over to where Jenny was hugging each child.

"These are my cousins."

When Shandra raised an eyebrow, she added. "They are the children of my cousins."

"This is the small village where my mother was raised. After she married, she moved to Kōloa and now Līhu'e. During my childhood, we came here often and I still love coming here." She had a child's hand in each of hers and walked toward a hut that was a larger than the rest. "This is my grandmother's home. She makes the best kā.lua. Pork that is roasted in the ground."

Shandra glanced over her shoulder at Ryan and smiled.

He nodded his head slightly.

They met Jenny and Leilani's grandmother.

"Does Leilani come here often?" Shandra asked. "This would be a wonderful place to find inspiration for art."

Jenny shook her head. "There was a time when she

came as much as me. The last few years, since becoming a member of the art society, she has had less and less time for family and her art."

"That's too bad. In college, she was always drawing and working on an art project. It was as if she had endless ideas." Shandra remembered how when she was at her lowest and couldn't think of a project to make for a class, Leilani had helped her see there was more than one way to express oneself with their art. They hadn't been close enough for Shandra to tell her classmate why she couldn't concentrate, but that didn't keep Leilani from helping.

"She has always seen beauty where others can't." Jenny passed the large wooden platter of roasted meat to them. "*E 'ai kākou*. Let's eat."

They filled their plates with the meat, pink sweet bread, Jenny told her was guava bread, and fruits.

"This is better than eating at any restaurant." Shandra took another bite of the salty, tasty meat.

"This is the best meal we've had since we arrived." Ryan put more meat on his plate.

"This is food made with love," Jenny said, smiling at her grandmother who sat at the end of the table watching them eat.

After the food had been cleared away, Ryan motioned for Jenny to follow him outside. Shandra figured they were going to talk about police stuff so she lingered, walking out the back door and studying the environment where their food had been prepared. It was a lean-to off the back of the hut. A long wood table was where the food was prepared. She spotted the hole in the ground where the meat had been cooked.

"You want to learn to cook in *imu*?" Jenny's

grandmother asked.

"What's an *imu*?" Shandra was thinking of the bird just smaller than an ostrich.

"It is the oven in the ground where the meat is cooked." The old woman led Shandra to the side of the hole in the ground. "Fire under the lava rocks, make them hot. Shredded banana stumps over the rocks make steam. The food is wrapped in banana and ti leaves. This gives it all flavor. This is tied with string and placed over the fire and covered with dirt. It cooks for five to twelve hours depending on how large an animal you are cooking."

"The banana and ti leaves are what give the meat such good flavor?" Shandra asked.

"It is the combination of all that is Kaua'i that makes our food delicious." The old woman smiled.

"Shandra? Are you ready?" Ryan called from the other side of the hut.

"Coming!" she called back and hugged the woman. "*Mahalo* for a wonderful meal and a lesson on Kaua'i cooking."

She hurried around the hut to the front. Jenny's car was gone. "Where did Jenny go?"

"To take her photos and our findings to Detective Kane and her contact at HIDTA." Ryan held the passenger door open for her. "Did you enjoy our lunch?"

"I did. You won't need to feed me for a couple of days."

Ryan laughed. "I doubt that."

When he sat behind the steering wheel, Shandra asked, "Are we going to see Elijah now?"

"Yes. We need to find out why he lied to us and

everyone else."

Chapter Eighteen

The large plantation style house over-looking the ocean would have been a pleasure to visit given other circumstances. Ryan parked the rental vehicle and walked with Shandra around the main house to the bungalow behind.

Rock music blared. The young painter had either gotten over his grief or was using painting as therapy.

Shandra hung back as Ryan opened the door and headed straight for the record player. Once the noise was turn off, he realized the artist wasn't painting. Ryan checked the back rooms. A bedroom, bath, and kitchenette. No one.

"Do you think he's in the main house?" Shandra asked, peering at the half-painted canvas on the easel.

"Either that or he's gone for a walk." He hadn't been gone long enough for the record to have finished. "You check in the main house. I'll go look around outside."

Shandra nodded and headed to the house. Ryan headed toward an opening in the brush and trees that revealed a narrow dirt path that was used often. He followed the path around the edge of the trees to the open area in front of the house.

He had to be down over the edge of the cliff for them to have not seen the young artist when they drove up. Ryan followed a path from the driveway toward the cliff edge. This wasn't as high off the shoreline as Patrick's studio.

Elijah stood just over the rim of the cliff, talking on a cell phone. His back was to the path leading up to him.

Ryan placed his feet carefully to not give away his approach. Within ten feet of the artist he stopped and listened.

"Why did you kill her?" The anguish in his voice said he was torn up over Billie's death. The hand he'd ran through his shoulder length hair fisted. "Don't you threaten me. I know everything. I want what you promised Patrick and double it to make up for taking Billie from me."

A rooster crowed from the brush to their left.

Elijah jumped and turned slightly. He swiped a finger across his phone and spun toward Ryan. "Are you looking for me?"

"Yes. We…well Shandra was looking for you in the main house. We have some questions for you." Ryan remained casual when he really wanted to grab the young man by his shirt front, give him a good shake, and haul him into Kane. But he couldn't let on he knew Elijah had been talking to the killer.

"Okay. I'll try. I'm pretty shook up about Billie."

He brushed by Ryan, walking back up the path.

Yeah, shook up enough to demand double whatever Patrick was getting. But for what?

As soon as they appeared on the top of the cliff, Shandra hurried down the path to them. "You found him."

Shandra stopped in front of Elijah. "How are you doing?"

The young artist shrugged.

"You and Billie were more than friends according to what Mrs. Kim told us last night. Why did you make us think otherwise?" Shandra wasn't giving the man any time to come up with distractions.

Ryan decided to let her lead the conversation and hear the answers before he let it be known he'd heard the phone conversation.

"I didn't think how Billie and I felt about one another was anyone's business but ours." Elijah picked up the pace headed for the side of the main house.

"Why was she pretending to hang out with Patrick and then sneak back here with you at night?" Shandra asked.

Ryan could tell by her tone she realized the young man was trying to dodge her questions.

Elijah swung around, facing them. "I'm grieving right now. Can these questions wait for another time?"

Ryan stepped around Shandra. "No. They can't. Two people are dead. You'll be the third if you don't come talk with Detective Kane and tell him everything you know about their deaths."

The young man's eyes widened. Fear and surprise registered on his face. "I can't go to the police." He stated and then stuttered, "I don't know anything."

"The phone call I overheard says you know enough to be the third victim." Ryan held out his hand. "Give me your phone."

"You aren't a policeman here. I don't have to." He spun around and ran to his studio.

"Call Kane, tell him Elijah knows who the killer is and I have him at this address," Ryan told Shandra and headed after the artist to make sure he remained in his bungalow until the detective arrived.

~*~

After talking to the detective and telling him what she knew, Shandra walked over to where Ryan stood, leaning against the wall of the bungalow.

"You sure he won't go out the back?"

He smiled. "I checked. There's no back door and the windows have bars on them. Mrs. Kim must have had vandals come in from the back at one time."

Shandra leaned against the wall on the other side of the door. "You know, he could be in there calling whoever you think he knows about and telling them we know."

"He's probably trying to figure out what to tell the detective when he arrives. I heard him tell the killer he wanted double what Patrick was going to get because he knew everything and Billie wasn't supposed to die." Ryan stared at her. "I think whatever Patrick was doing for money was set-up by Elijah. Now he has two deaths on his conscience."

"You would think he'd come forward with the name. Especially if Billie wasn't supposed to die." Shandra shivered. Billie's boyfriend talked her into doing something that must have been illegal for her and Patrick to have ended up dead. Here she'd been angry with Brendan for using Francie, but the woman's eyes were wide open and she knew the consequences for being a paid escort. While Billie had helped Elijah out of love and had paid the hardest price. He was more of a user than Brendan.

"Hey. Don't worry, Kane will take him into custody and he'll be safe," Ryan said from his side of the door.

She smiled. He had no idea where her thoughts had gone. It was a good thing. She didn't care to share them.

The door opened.

Elijah took one step out, saw both of them and jumped back, slamming the door shut.

About that time, they spotted Detective Kane and two uniformed officers come around the side of the main house.

"You'll need his phone to get the number of who he was talking to," Ryan said, meeting the detective twenty feet from the door. Shandra had followed her husband.

"You say he was talking to the killer?" Kane stared at Ryan, flicked a glance at her, and then settled his full attention on her husband.

"I overheard his conversation. He was mad whoever it was had killed Billie. He said that wasn't supposed to happen and he wanted double Patrick's money to make up for Billie's death." Ryan shot a quick glance at the bungalow. "He knows who the murderer is."

The detective motioned to the officers. They took up the spots on each side of the door.

Detective Kane walked up to the door and

pounded. "Elijah Lee, this is Detective Kane with the Līhu'e Police. I'm asking you to come out of your own accord or I'll send in officers to drag you out."

The door opened and Elijah stepped out.

One officer cuffed him.

"Why are you treating me like a criminal?" the young man accused.

"You were overheard talking with the person responsible for two deaths. You are an accomplice to those deaths." Detective Kane stared at the artist until he dropped his gaze to the ground.

One of the officers frisked Elijah. He came up with a wallet, chap stick, change, and a paint rag. No phone.

"Where's your phone?" the detective asked.

The young man shrugged.

"Put him in the car." When the two officers escorted the artist toward the front of the property, Detective Kane motioned to Shandra and Ryan. "Let's find his phone. If I have the number and discover the name, it will be a lot easier to make him talk."

Shandra let the detective and Ryan enter the bungalow first. They were looking at all the usual places someone might hide a phone. She started looking through the art supplies, between the canvases stacked against a wall, and even the pile of dirty paint rags in a bucket.

Ryan came out of the bathroom. "I didn't find it in here."

Detective Kane walked out of the bedroom. "Nothing here either. I'll try the kitchenette."

Shandra stood in the middle of the studio. So far, the young man had proven cunning. While he put on a naïve act, he had orchestrated something that was to make his friend money. And he'd managed to be taken care of by a wealthy widow.

"I'm going to take a look around outside," she said to no one in particular since both men were banging around in the kitchen.

He'd tried to come out of the bungalow, but they'd been there. If he hadn't put his phone in the toilet, he might have dropped it outside the window, hoping to retrieve it later.

She walked to the back of the building and smiled. The bars were wide enough he could have reached through and tossed the phone away from the window. The bars on the narrow bathroom window seemed senseless. The only other window that he could have used was the bedroom.

Walking to stand in front of the window, she faced the jungle beyond and started a back and forth search from the window into the bushes and trees. The nasty little biting fly that lurked in the damp sunless areas of the forest had her slapping her arms, neck, and legs as she tried to concentrate on the ground.

She slapped her left leg and stepped with her right. Something hard and square was under her foot. She raised it up and spotted the corner of a phone. Scooping it off the ground, she headed out of the forest as fast as she could, ignoring the stinging bites.

"I found it!" she called, walking to the front of the bungalow.

Both men strode out the door. Ryan first. He stopped in front of her.

She held the phone by two fingers and scratched at her legs with her other hand.

"Where did you find it?" Detective Kane asked,

taking it in his gloved hand and dropping it into an evidence bag.

"About twenty feet into the jungle behind the bedroom window." She peered into her husband's eyes. "He couldn't get out, but his arm could and he tossed the phone."

"How did you think to look there?" the detective asked, staring at her with narrowed eyes.

"If we didn't find it in the bungalow and you didn't find it on him, he had to get it out of the house. We were standing at the front. He knew that because he opened the door, looked at us, and went back in." She now used both hands to rub up and down her arms and legs. "It only made sense he threw it out of the house, knowing it was the only thing that would connect him to the murders."

"I'm getting you back to Leilani's for an oatmeal bath," Ryan said, taking her by the arm and leading her around the pool.

"Jump in there. It's a saltwater pool. It will help take the burn of the stings away. But if you've scratched up skin, it will burn." The detective's tone almost sounded as if he cared she was uncomfortable.

"I'll wait for the oatmeal bath."

Chapter Nineteen

Ryan paced back and forth as Shandra submerged herself in the large jacuzzi tub in Leilani's master bathroom.

"Kane should have called by now. He should have figured out who the number belonged to on Elijah's phone."

Shandra glanced up at her agitated husband. "You know if he found out who the person is, he'll have to question Elijah and get something solid before he can go after them." Sometimes she wondered how her husband managed to hold it together on the other cases they'd worked together.

"That's true. But the longer it takes for him to gather the information, the more time the murderer has to get away." Ryan sat on the edge of the tub. "Are you feeling less itchy?"

She sighed. "Yes! I'm glad you thought of stopping at a drug store and getting Epsom salt and the oatmeal soak. Those are nasty little bugs." She was also glad Jenny had insisted they put on the bug spray the day before when they climbed down the cliff and found the cave.

"Did Detective Kane have any time to tell you if they'd learned anything about the box in the cave?" She picked up a washcloth and smoothed it down her legs.

"He only said the drug task force was looking into it." Ryan frowned.

She knew that look. He wasn't happy with the answer he was given.

"I left a message with Jenny. I want to see if she's learned anything. And if she knows if Elijah would have any connections with drug dealers." Ryan's phone buzzed. "It's her. I'll talk to her in the living room so you can finish in peace." He opened the bathroom door. "Hello?"

Shandra watched him walk through the bedroom and out the next door. So much for hearing his side of the conversation. She finished soaking, dried off, smeared oatmeal-based lotion all over her arms and legs, dressed, and entered the living room.

Ryan sat on the couch, her sketch pad on his lap.

"Have you taken up drawing?" she asked, sitting next to him.

He had a list of names and a list of what they knew.

"Didn't Jenny have any good news?" Shandra read the names. *Darnell, Southwell, Lee*. "Are these people Jenny named as knowing drug dealers?"

He shook his head. "Jenny is meeting someone tonight. Said it took her all day to get in contact with him. I'm going with her." He held up a hand when Shandra started to protest. "I need you and Leilani to go to the gallery and see if you can find anything out of place with Southwell and Lee's things. Or anything there that could be tied to Darnell."

"Why do you think Saul has anything to do with this?" Shandra didn't care for the artist, but he'd been genuinely shocked at finding Billie dead.

"Jenny told me he owns a boat. The kind that can go fast and get away from the Coast Guard *and* is small enough to fit in the cave we found." Ryan peered into her eyes. "You should be safe. Go after the gallery is closed and lock the door once you get in."

"And you? Will you be safe?" She put a hand on his arm.

"Jenny knows the guy and says he isn't the one we're looking for, but he talked like he knew something about the deaths." Ryan put his hand on top of hers. "And I'm telling all of this to Kane before Jenny picks me up."

"Why not now?" Shandra asked.

Ryan tapped the pencil on the pad. "Because I don't want him getting to the guy before we do. I have a feeling Jenny's friend won't talk to the local cops. Jenny is going to introduce me as another P.I." He smiled at her. "Don't worry. I'm doing this fully legit. I'm just a plus one with Jenny to talk to a drug dealer."

She shook her head. "I know you lived that life undercover in Chicago, but that doesn't mean someone here in Kaua'i won't be able to tell you're a policeman."

"I'll be fine. And so will you. After finding that phone today, I have a feeling you'll know what to look for in the gallery."

He had more faith in her abilities than she did.

~*~

After texting Leilani and telling her to wait at the gallery for her when it closed, Shandra saw Ryan off with Jenny. Leilani's cousin promised she wouldn't let anything happen to Ryan. But to remember he was a big boy who knew how to handle himself.

Shandra reminded herself of that every day when he headed to work as a Weippe County Detective. But this was different. He was walking into a meeting with a drug dealer. Not that they didn't have some in Weippe County, they were just small stuff, nothing like she was sure they would meet tonight.

She fixed a salad and sat down to stare at Ryan's list. After his explanation of Saul, she understood his and Elijah's names. But Brendan Darnell. Was it because he needed money? Putting the salad down, Shandra picked up her laptop and started searching Brendan Darnell, Kaua'i Hawaii. What she wanted to know specifically; Did he own a boat capable of running drugs? He didn't. He had a yacht that was up for sale. So was his property in Hanalei and Princeville. It appeared he was selling off everything but the family estate. He was in need of money more than the starving artists who could work the art community to get handouts and places to stay.

Photos of Brendan and Francie were all over the Kaua'i social pages on the internet. Francie said Brendan was going to let her go. He couldn't afford her. She looked happy, clinging to his arm in all the photos. Would she try to help him make money to keep her? She hadn't sounded like she'd cared to stay. Judging from the smiles in the photos, she was a very good actress.

Shandra tucked that thought away to ask Leilani about when they met. Her friend had asked why she needed to stay at the gallery after closing. Shandra had been evasive. She knew her friend hadn't killed anyone, but she didn't want Leilani to accidently say something to the wrong person.

Rather than sit around here waiting for two more hours, Shandra put her laptop away, grabbed her purse and the rental car keys, and headed to the gallery.

~*~

Expecting to meet the drug dealer in some bar or estate, Ryan was surprised as he walked behind Jenny through the gates of a closed botanical garden.

"This is where we're meeting your friend?" Ryan asked.

Jenny tossed a smile over her shoulder and continued walking down the path between plants Ryan knew his wife would love to draw. The colors and fragrances were an overload for his eyes and nose.

They skirted the visitor center and headed to a greenhouse beyond. The moisture and heat level today had been tolerable. Inside the hothouse, Ryan was surprised to see a tall thin man sitting in a lawn chair, sipping a cold drink. There wasn't a bead of sweat on his long thin face.

The man's eyes lit up at the sight of Jenny. "*Kaikamahine*, I was surprised by your call."

Jenny grasped the man's outstretched hands. "You know I only call when I need someone smarter than me." She kissed his cheek and stepped back, motioning to Ryan. "This is another P.I. His client is mixed up with mine so we are working together."

Ryan watched the man, studying him. When the

man nodded, Ryan reached out to shake hands.

"Have a seat." The man clapped his hands together and a young man appeared with two folding chairs.

Jenny took the chair closest to the man. "What do you know about drugs being transferred in wet caves?"

The man's gaze flicked from Jenny to Ryan and back to the woman. "You have a client who needs to know this?"

"I have a client who wishes to find the truth." She indicated Ryan. "He has a client who wishes to know who killed their family member. We both believe it has to do with drugs and a wet cave."

The man picked his cold drink back up and snapped the fingers on his empty hand.

The same young man returned with two cold drinks for them.

Ryan wanted to press the cold glass with condensation to his forehead but didn't want to act like an outsider.

"I have heard there was someone new trying to get a hold on the island." The man studied Jenny. "Is this anything to do with your past profession?"

Ryan wondered how well Jenny could lie. This had everything to do with helping the police find the murder of two people.

"A small amount. I have been talking to the police to learn information." She shifted closer to the man. "I know you heard about the artist who fell off the cliff at Halekoa Point. The police believe my cousin, Leilani, did it. It's my family I am gathering information for."

The man nodded. "I heard and saw your cousin was mentioned with the death. I see why you are digging so hard." He sipped his drink and glanced at

Ryan. "And you. Why do you need to know?"

Ryan smiled. "Money. I discover who killed the artist and I get paid." He'd learned how to deal with the underworld during his days undercover in Chicago. He didn't care to go back to that life or relive any of those two years during and after. But he could slip into that life with ease.

The man studied him, grinned back, and motioned to Jenny. "You might want to keep an eye on him. He could dig up dirt on Leilani to get what he wants."

Jenny scowled at the older man and then at him.

Ryan gave her a half smirk. "We both want the truth. If it's your cousin, I'm sorry."

"Who has been moving meth onto the island?" Jenny asked, now blunt and to the point.

It appeared she didn't care for how easily he'd fallen in with the drug dealer.

"No name. Someone with contacts in Mexico. I do know it has been concentrated in the Kōloa area." The man sipped his drink. "You might try bars in Kōloa and Līhuʻe. The ones that don't have bouncers." He studied Jenny for several seconds.

It was obvious he was telling her the places with bouncers were dealing his drugs. Ryan wondered if Kane and the drug task force knew about the dealings.

"Thanks for the help." Jenny stood, finished off her drink, and motioned for Ryan to follow.

He pushed out of the chair. "Pleasure meeting you. If you're ever in need of a P.I. tell Jenny to get in touch with me."

Outside, walking back to the gate, Jenny said quietly, "What was that all about. He'll never contact you."

"You and I know that, but if he thinks I'm a money grubbing P.I. that's what he would have expected me to say." Ryan walked over to Jenny's car. "I've messed with his kind before. You never go out of character when you work them."

"Note taken. You were undercover for how long?" she asked, starting the vehicle.

"Too long." There were few things in his life he'd like to do over. Agreeing to go undercover in Chicago was one he would change.

Chapter Twenty

An hour before the gallery closed, Shandra walked through the door. There were two couples slowly browsing the artwork. One couple were in their seventies and the other in their thirties, she guessed. Leilani stood behind the counter, tapping on the computer keyboard.

"Hey, I was bored sitting around so I came in early," she said, approaching the counter.

Leilani jumped, her eyes focused, and she smiled. "Sorry. I was deep in thought."

Shandra studied her friend. Anxious wasn't the right word, but she was definitely worried. "What were you thinking about?"

"This whole thing." She lowered her voice. "What it will do to the event and the art society."

"You think the deaths will hurt the art society? How?" Shandra walked around the counter, so they could converse in quieter tones. No sense her friend's worries getting to the ears of patrons.

Leilani hit the power button on the computer and sat.

Shandra wondered if it was to keep her from seeing something or just her friend's way of showing she wanted to give Shandra her full attention.

"Two artists, one who was rejected and one who made the show, have been murdered. That doesn't look good. Artist aren't going to want to put their work in the show next year. And sponsors…we are a non-profit. We depend on others to promote and sponsor the prizes. Not just art enthusiasts, but businesses."

"I'm sure once the killer is brought to justice and everyone learns why the murders were committed, you'll be able to smooth things over." Shandra caught a glimpse of the older couple headed to the door. "Thank you for coming in!" she called out in a genial tone.

The man smiled and raised a hand in a wave.

The younger couple had been hidden in the corner behind a false wall for a long time. "Just a minute," Shandra said in a low voice to Leilani. She stood and strode to that area, quietly crossing the carpeted floor.

The two were messing with one of Saul's paintings.

"Excuse me, but you can't touch the artwork," she said loudly.

The two jumped. Their faces bright red.

"We were, just—just seeing how it was hooked to the wall," the man said, pushing the woman in the opposite direction.

"Just like all the others. Why were you really messing with the painting?" Shandra now stood in front of it.

"We told you." The man grasped the woman by the hand, and they headed straight for the door.

"What's going on?" Leilani asked, appearing in the corner.

"They were looking behind Saul's painting." Shandra reached up and took it off the wall. She spun it around and didn't see anything. Replacing it on the wall, she noticed that the paintings to the right of that photo were all a bit crooked. As if they had been looked behind.

There were two more small paintings by Saul on the left and one by Jonas Nakamura. "Straighten those while I look at these," she said to Leilani. Both of Saul's paintings had nothing. But three small packets of what looked like the crystals they'd found in the chest in the cave were taped to the bottom board of the canvas on Jonas' painting.

"What is that?" Leilani asked, when she'd finished straightening the paintings and peered over Shandra's shoulder.

"Ice." When her friend stared at her expressionless, she added, "It's a drug called Meth. Someone is selling it from this exhibit." She stared at her friend. "Who else was working here today?"

"I came in mid-afternoon. Celia was here. She stayed on for about an hour. We were discussing the deaths and how it might influence next year's show. And it's been just me since she left." Leilani's eyes widened. "Do you think this is what Patrick was supposed to do and he backed out?"

"Why would you say that?" Shandra asked.

Leilani pointed at the painting. Of all the paintings in the area, the one she'd found the "ice" on had the most red paint.

"But how could he have had his painting put back here, in this corner?" Shandra asked.

"The award-winning paintings go up front. That's why he didn't bring one of his other paintings. He brought one that he was sure would be put back here."

An idea struck. "No. He got cold feet and brought a painting he knew wouldn't make the exhibit. Instead of saying he wouldn't allow whoever it was to put drugs behind his painting, he painted something that wouldn't make it into the exhibition." Shandra stared at Leilani. "His blaming you for it not making it was a show. Whoever had asked him to help sell drugs must have been here Wednesday night. When they saw his painting didn't make it, he was killed so he couldn't tell anyone about the plan."

She replaced the painting and pulled Leilani to the desk. "Go lock the door. We don't want anyone else to come in." Shandra picked up her phone and dialed the Līhu'e Police Department and asked to speak with Detective Kane.

~*~

Ryan shoved himself out of Jenny's car. This was the third bar tonight. He was tired and thinking the man had given them a tale to keep them away from his dealings.

"Do you really think we'll learn anything here?" he asked as they walked up to the entrance.

Jenny stopped and smiled. "You know it's footwork that finds the leads. Come on. You'll like this one."

The atmosphere in this bar was definitely Hawaiian. The music, the open-air walls, grass skirts

142

for lamp shades, and waitresses walking around in bikini bottoms and coconut shell tops with a sarong tied around their waists.

The clientele appeared to be more islanders than vacationers. The last two places had definitely catered to the tourists.

Jenny walked up to the bar. "Hey Pila, two beers, please."

The man around their age smiled and winked. "Ah, I knew you would come back to visit me."

"I might have come to see you and I might not." She looped her arm around Ryan's.

The man frowned. "You know, every time you bring a date in here you break my heart."

"Pila, if your wife heard you, she'd be breaking something other than your heart."

He laughed and slid two beers across the bar. Ryan paid for them and picked them up. They found a table in the corner and he studied her.

"You two seem to have a history?" He sipped the beer and moved his attention to the crowd milling about.

"He's my ex. We split up because he was sleeping with a barmaid. He married her. Now she stays home with the kids and he mans the bar and flirts. And most likely is sleeping with another barmaid."

Ryan caught her chugging her drink. "And you're not over him."

She smiled sheepishly. "Why is it we women always fall for the bad boy when there's a nice man willing to marry us?"

Ryan thought about Shandra's first lover. "Yeah, it seems all women have to try a bad boy once." He took a sip of his beer. "But there is always the nice guy there to pick up the pieces."

"You the one who picked up Shandra's pieces?"

He shook his head. "No. She had herself picked up and kicking ass when I met her. I think you're a lot alike. Go say 'yes' to the nice guy in your life. I think you've gotten yourself back together."

Jenny laughed. "Thanks for the pep talk." She tipped the top of her glass ever so slightly. "That guy over there has been slipping little by little into heavier criminal activity."

The guy he presumed she meant without full-out staring, was in his late twenties, wearing board shorts, a tank top that showed off powerful arms and chest, and flipflops. His hair was cut military short. For some reason, Ryan found that unexpected, given his attire and what Jenny had said about him.

Then the man faced the other direction, laughing with two women, and Ryan saw the nasty scar on the back of his head.

"How'd that happen? The scar."

"Surfboard accident when he was a teenager. He thinks it makes him tough to keep his hair short and show it off." Jenny's disgusted tone drew Ryan's attention.

"Surfboard accidents aren't some kind of a step up the surfing hierarchy like a cowboy getting bucked off a horse that's never been rode?"

She snorted. "If it had been a legitimate accident maybe. He said something another surfer didn't like and that person bashed him over the head."

"I see. It was his attitude and mouth that got that scar, not a big wave."

She nodded. "Ahh, he just slipped something from his hand into that blonde's. Go start talking with her and see if you can find out what it was. I can't go over because he knows me."

Ryan picked up his drink and wound his way slowly toward the young woman, keeping his gaze locked on her.

By the time he'd caught up to her, the young man had moved on to another group of young women.

Ryan bumped into the woman. "I'm sorry. This place is packed."

She frowned at him. Her gaze shifted to his hands in air as if he had tried to avoid the collision. She smiled. "It's always like this. You a tourist? I haven't seen you around here before." She slipped onto a tall chair at a table next to her.

"I'm from off the island," he said, standing beside her chair.

"You can have a seat. My friend is busy dancing." She kicked the empty chair away from the table.

"Thanks." Ryan sat, took a sip of his beer and glanced Jenny's direction. She was talking to another man close to her age.

"You here with someone?" The blonde followed his gaze.

"My cousin. She's kind of on a date, but she met the guy on the internet and wanted me to hang around and keep an eye on things." It felt like a flimsy excuse, but the blonde's eyes lit up.

"That's so sweet! I don't think my cousin would do that for me." She sipped her drink. It was a fruity one with a little umbrella. "So far has he seemed like a normal guy?"

"Yeah. But sometimes those are the ones you have to watch out for. They don't show their stripes until later." He smiled and sipped his beer.

Her eyes narrowed. "Are you trying to tell me, you're someone I should watch out for?"

She wasn't as naïve as she appeared.

"No. Just stating not all guys are what they appear."

She glanced at his left hand. "I see you're married."

He wiggled his fingers and smiled. "That I am. Happily."

"Happy because she lets you out to go to bars?" The young woman placed her mouth on the straw sticking out of her drink.

"Happy because she understands family duty and loves me." He tipped his head in the direction of the thug the young woman had been talking to. "He your date?"

Her cheeks darkened, and she patted her small purse dangling from a string across her body. "No. Just an acquaintance."

"An acquaintance that supplies you with drugs?"

"Hey." Her eyes narrowed and her voice lowered. "Are you a cop?"

"Not here. Back in the states. Hard to miss an exchange. What is he dealing?" He peered into her eyes. "I'm not here to bust you. But if you're smart, like I think you are, you'll lay off that stuff."

She stared back, licked her lips, and reached into her purse. She slid the packet across to him. "Ice. He's been selling it here every night since I arrived." The woman scanned the bar. "Are you sure you aren't going to arrest me?"

"Yes, I can't. I told you, I'm a cop from off the island. But I am working with an island cop on something else." He tucked the packet into his pocket. "Don't tell anyone about this."

"Is your cousin the other cop?"

"Nope. Thanks." He picked up his drink and walked across the floor to where Jenny sat with the man who'd taken his place when he left.

"Ryan, I'd like you to meet Charlie Hart. He's with HIDTA." Jenny slid over, making room for Ryan in the booth beside her.

He sat and nodded at the man. Was he here watching the young man? In which case he should know the surfer was dealing.

"I saw you and the blonde were talking. She handed you something, what was it?" Hart asked.

Ryan glanced at Jenny.

She nodded.

"It was a packet of Ice she bought from the surfer."

The man studied him. "You want me to take him in for questioning?"

"Not yet. I'm giving it to Kane to see if it matches what we found earlier. I'd like to know if he's mixed up in the deaths before we arrest him."

Hart nodded. "We don't get many murders on this island. Everyone would like to get them cleared up quickly."

Ryan's phone buzzed. He glanced at the text. *Det. Kane at gallery. Something happened.* He stood. "Jenny, we need to go. She'll let you know what to do when we know."

Chapter Twenty-one

The detective had arrived quicker than Shandra had expected. The big man now stood in front of the counter as two forensics personnel took photos and fingerprints on the painting with the drugs hidden behind it.

"You say, only you and this Celia Niau worked here today?" the detective questioned Leilani.

"Yes. Here is the schedule for this week and the rest of the month." Leilani handed over a page she'd photocopied from the one that hung on a small bulletin board in the tiny room in the back that worked as a breakroom/closet. "Every artist who has work in the exhibit has to take a turn manning the exhibit. It not only makes it so we don't have to pay anyone, it gives the people who come in access to the artists to talk about their work."

Shandra had to give Leilani credit, she was a walking billboard for the art society. She understood her friend's fears of losing this exhibition and possibly the society. Which gave her even less motive to have done anything to hurt what she was so adamant about keeping alive.

"A different person opens the door every day." The detective studied Leilani. "Do you all have a key?"

"No. I have one, because I come and go all the time taking care of matters, but the person who is opening, goes to the mall office and mall security opens the door for them. I'm usually here most nights and I lock up." Leilani stared at the computer screen. "But I think Brendan Darnell asked for a key to the gallery. As the Chairman of the art society, he felt he should have access when he wanted."

Shandra watched the detective. He didn't flinch or even act as if that was odd. She thought it was. Why would he need unlimited access to the gallery? And he was one of her top suspects in the murders.

"Kane, tell this officer I'm allowed in."

Ryan's voice at the door shot Shandra to her feet. Her gaze met her husband's. Relief eased the lines on his face.

"Let him in," Detective Kane said, gruffly. He glanced at Shandra. "I suppose you contacted him?"

"Yes."

Ryan walked straight to Shandra and pulled her into a hug. "Are you okay?" he whispered.

"Yes." She gently detached herself from his arms. "I discovered a painting was being used to exchange Ice."

Ryan faced the detective. "You have samples then?"

"Yes." The detective studied Ryan. "Why?"

He reached into his pants pocket and held out a small packet like the ones she'd found behind the painting. "You might want to see if they match the batch this came from. If it does, Jenny can tell you the name of the person who was distributing this." He plopped it into the evidence bag one of the forensics officers brought over.

"Where did you get that?" Detective Kane asked, taking the evidence bag and poising a pen over it.

"At the Kaua'i Luau Bar. A young lady purchased it from the dealer. She said he's been there every night for the last six days. She's visiting. The bartender, Pila, said he's been in nightly for the last five months. A HIDTA officer was there. I told him I was handing it over to you. I had planned on you matching it to the chest we found in the cave."

Shandra saw the dark cloud that crossed the detective's face.

"There wasn't a chest of Ice when we went to the cave you told us about."

"Damn! That means they picked it up between the time we found it and you arrived. How long after I told you did you send someone to get it?" Ryan looked as perturbed as the detective.

"By the time we gathered people it was a good ten hours."

Ryan ran a hand over the back of his neck. He was getting as embroiled in this case as if it was one of his own back in Weippe County.

"Do you think someone learned we had found the chest or they just came in at their scheduled time to get it?" Shandra asked, glancing between the two men.

They both shrugged.

"Oh no!" Leilani moaned.

"What's wrong?" Shandra glanced back at her friend who had been quiet since Ryan arrived.

"There's a reporter out there. We don't need drugs added to the two deaths. This exhibition and possibly the art society could be in jeopardy." She looked defeated.

"Ms. Brown, I really need to finish your statement." Detective Kane glanced at Shandra. "Maybe you could go say something to the reporter. But nothing about anything we've found out about the murders or the possible link to drugs."

Shandra stared at the man. "What credence will anything I have to say have with the reporter?"

"You're the judge, aren't you?" He shifted his attention to Leilani.

Shandra glanced at her husband. He gave her a smile and waved to the door.

She tried to form a comment as she crossed the room to the door. Once there, she dropped the thought as the reporter snapped a photo of her behind the door, with a policeman standing guard.

Shoving out the door, she stopped in front of the reporter. "Can I help you?"

"You're the judge for this art exhibition that has turned into a melodrama." The reporter, a young woman, didn't even really ask a question.

"I was asked to juror this exhibition."

"And one of the artists you didn't allow into the exhibition was killed. Do you have anything to say about that?"

"I can't predict what will happen to people. His death had nothing to do with this art show." Shandra didn't like the smirk on the woman's face.

"Then why was there an emergency meeting called? One at which you presided."

She racked her memory trying to remember if this woman had been anywhere near when they had the meeting. She stared at her long dark hair, round face, and digging brown eyes. No, she was sure of it. "How did you find out about the meeting?"

"I have my sources. You were also present when the body of another artist, one who made the exhibition, was found. How do you explain that?"

She knew for certain this woman wasn't anywhere near Saul's house when they found the body. "I don't need to explain that to you."

"And here you are, when drugs have been found in the gallery. I'm beginning to think you may be bad for this art society and this island." The woman raised her brows and poised her pen over a pad.

"I'd like to know your name, who you work for?" Shandra said.

They stared at one another for several minutes. The woman spun around and walked away.

Shandra asked the officer, "Did she give a name or the newspaper she works for?"

"No."

She entered the gallery. Leilani was walking to the back room.

"What did you say?" Ryan asked.

"Nothing. She knew too much to be a reporter. And she didn't give me a name or who she works for. I want to know how Leilani knew she was a reporter." She followed her friend to the back room.

Leilani sat in the dark, her head in her hands,

sobbing.

"Hey. This isn't that bad," Shandra said, dropping into a plastic chair next to her.

"What did you say?" Leilani asked, wiping at the tears.

"Nothing. Was she really a reporter?"

That caught her friend's attention. "What do you mean?"

"She was making vicious accusations and knew too much of what had been going on even for a reporter. Someone has been feeding her information."

Leilani's hands fisted. "Damn him! Brendan has been trying to make this society a for profit. I've been able to convince people that it is better to keep it non-profit. If he can prove to the other board members that I am incapable of running this, he'll get his wish."

"I don't understand. Why would he want to make if for profit? What would he gain?"

"An income. If he can make it for profit and remain the chairman, he would be paid." Leilani sighed. "Then we would all have to do things the way he wanted instead of a majority vote by the board. That is why I want to keep it non-profit."

"But does he know everything that has been happening here? I mean, how would he have known about the drugs in here tonight to have sent the reporter?" Shandra wondered if the man was cagier than he'd acted thus far.

"The only explanation would be if he put the drugs here himself." Leilani picked up her purse.

~*~

Ryan stood beside Kane hashing out what the detective had learned from Shandra and Leilani.

"The couple Shandra found looking for the drugs had to have paid someone and been told to come here." It was an odd way to distribute drugs. And for the people to pay money and believe whoever they paid would have the drugs waiting for them here.

"I don't get it." Ryan stared at the detective. He seemed to be thinking something through as well.

"We'll get hold of the surveillance tapes for the mall and see if we can I.D. the couple and find out why they were looking under the paintings." Kane leveled his gaze on Ryan. "Either Ms. Brown is a very good liar or she hasn't a clue what is going on around here. Your wife is the one that noticed the couple spending extra time in this corner. She came to check it out and found the couple messing with a painting." Kane pointed to the largest painting in the middle. "They weren't even looking under the right painting. This is all the strangest case I've ever had."

"I'm grabbing Shandra and following Leilani home. Maybe you'll have something in the morning. Either surveillance tapes or if those drugs are the same." Ryan shifted to leave.

"Keep an eye out. I'm getting the feeling someone is out to discredit Ms. Brown. Nothing else adds up."

Ryan nodded and headed to the empty counter.

Shandra and Leilani stepped out of the room in the back.

"Come on. Let's all go back to your house," he said, putting an arm around his wife and Leilani. His wife because he felt like holding her close. The other woman because she looked like she was about to fall apart.

"Why don't you drive Leilani and I'll follow

behind," Ryan offered.

Shandra kissed his cheek. "That's a great idea." She handed him the keys to the rental and walked with Leilani over to her car.

Once Shandra was in the driver's seat, Ryan slid into the rental and pulled up behind them as they left the parking lot.

He wasn't letting that car out of his sight. If Kane was correct, someone could still be out to hurt Leilani. He wasn't about to let anything happen to his wife or her friend.

Chapter Twenty-two

Driving through the tree tunnel from Līhuʻe to Kōloʻa, Shandra noticed a car close to the backend of the rental car. Why would anyone drive that close? They could easily go around. There was light traffic this time of night. She also noticed that Ryan drove close enough to Leilani's car to not allow the car to go around him and in between them.

This put her on alert. Ryan was worried someone might try to do something. Had he and Detective Kane come up with the same thought as Leilani? That someone was out to get her.

"Leilani, did you tell anyone you were going to see Patrick the night he died?" Shandra wondered if this was not only about discrediting her but perhaps framing her for the murder.

Her friend had been staring out the side window. She peered forward. "I might have said something to Billie. She stayed and helped me clean up." She shifted sideways. "Yes, I did tell her. Because I asked her why she wasn't off checking on Patrick since they had been seeing so much of each other lately. She said, she'd go around in the morning. That when he was mad, she didn't like to be around him."

"And that's when you said you were going to go check on him?" Shandra asked.

"Yes. I said something like someone should check on him. I guess it will be me." Leilani shoved hair off her face. "Do you think Billie told someone?"

"I'm sure of it." She wasn't going to tell her friend who. The less she knew the better.

They turned off the highway and onto the main road into Kōloa. The car that had been tailgating Ryan went on down the highway. Shandra let out a whoosh of relief and continued to Leilani's house.

She pulled into the driveway and hit the button to open the garage door. The door went up and she drove in. Believing Ryan would use the garage to access the house, she didn't push the button to close the door.

They climbed out of the car and Leilani headed for the door to the house.

"I'll wait here for Ryan. He was right behind us." Shandra stood at the side of the car.

Leilani nodded and continued into the house.

Ryan walked into the garage.

A scream echoed out of the house and into the stillness of the night.

"Close the garage door and wait here," Ryan ordered, rushing around her and into the house.

She hit the button, waited until the garage door was to the ground, and ran into the house.

Leilani stood in the entryway to her workroom.

Shandra peeked over her friend's shoulder.

Ryan stood inside the room on the phone. All of the partial and finished pottery had been broken into pieces. There were marks on the wall where the pieces had been thrown. Even her pottery wheel was broken.

After shoving his phone in his pocket, Ryan walked to the door, grabbed Leilani by the arm, and hauled her into the living room. "You need to tell me what you haven't so far. What do you know that has someone threatening you?"

Shandra had to agree with her husband, but she didn't like his tactics. "I'll make us all some tea." She started to stand and had second thoughts. "Ryan, why don't you make us some tea."

When he raised an eyebrow, she tipped her head toward the kitchen. He reluctantly walked that direction.

"It's obvious that Ryan called the police. Do you want to stay home and be protected or be taken to jail as a person of interest in two murders and a drug smuggling operation?" Shandra only waited a beat. "It's obvious by the mess in your workroom that someone is sending you a message."

Leilani stared at her hands, wringing in her lap. "I was in Patrick's bedroom one night when Billie and Elijah came by. Patrick didn't say anything about me being there so I stayed in the room." She glanced up. "I listened at the door."

"What were they talking about?"

Leilani drew in a deep breath and started. "A way that Patrick could make money and not have to be indebted to Brendan. Somehow Elijah knew that Brendan was about broke. He told Patrick to back out of his deal with him and they, he and Billie, I presumed, had a way for him to make all the money he needed and still have time to paint."

Shandra nodded. She'd believed the two had been behind something. That was why they'd pretended to have had a falling out. "Did you hear what?"

"Not really. When Patrick started painting that awful painting, I asked him what he was doing. He said, guaranteeing painting was in his future." She shook her head as Ryan walked into the room with a tray holding three mugs, a sugar pot, and spoons.

He placed the tray on the coffee table and sat down by Shandra. She placed three spoons of sugar in a cup, stirred, and handed it to Leilani.

"Did he ask you to make sure that painting made the show?" Shandra urged.

"He did. And then, later, he said he would let things fall as they may. Which was poetic for Patrick." She half smiled and sipped the tea. "Then when he yelled at me that it was all my fault he didn't get in the show, I was surprised, bewildered, and afraid. I didn't understand. If he had wanted me to make sure it was in the show, he should have told me. Why had he acted like it didn't matter then yell at me?"

Ryan picked up a cup of tea, nudging Shandra as he did so.

She peered into his eyes and mouthed, listen.

"So when Billie didn't plan on going to check on him, you decided to?" she said, filling in Ryan a bit. "And you're sure you didn't talk to Patrick or see anyone when you were there?" Shandra asked as the doorbell rang.

Ryan rose to answer the door.

It had to be the police. She wanted to get all of Leilani's story before anyone else attempted.

Tears dripped down Leilani's face, sliding down her pointed chin and landing in her tea cup. "I did talk to him." She swiped at the tears with the hand not holding the mug of tea. "In his studio. He was pacing back and forth when I arrived. I asked him why he hadn't asked me to make sure the painting made the exhibition. He said because he didn't want me to get involved. That I needed to get away from him and stay away from him. I asked him why. He said because he'd deposited the money given to him for his agreeing to help. But he didn't like what he had to do and backed out. They were going to want their money back. Then he said go away. He had to think and he headed to the cliff. I walked out, got in my car, and it was when I was turning around, I saw him go over the edge. I thought he'd jumped. I ran from my car and tried to get to him, but in the dark without a flashlight, I couldn't see anything. Then the shock." She put the tea down and grasped Shandra's hands. "If I had been strong enough, do you think I could have saved him if I'd called for help?"

Shandra shook her head. "Whoever wanted him dead had most likely already hit him with the rock by the time you tried to reach him."

"That's a relief. I've been torturing myself that my shock cost him his life."

Ryan and Detective Kane entered the living room. Shandra could tell by the looks on their faces they'd stood back listening.

The detective walked forward and grasped the chair, placing it to face the couch. He sat. "Leilani. You know something. There is no other explanation for all that has happened today. What can you tell me about that night? Before you said the lights had been off in the studio. You know that because?"

"They weren't off. I'd left them on for Patrick to use to find his way back to the studio. There was a sliver of moon that night and a bit overcast. It was dark." She picked up her tea and sipped it. "I talked to Patrick." She went on to tell him everything she'd told Shandra.

"This Billie, who you told about checking on Patrick. Is it the same person as the Billie who visited with Elijah?" Detective Kane asked.

"Yes. She's also dead." Leilani wiped at a tear that escaped her left eye.

The detective glanced up at Shandra. She nodded.

"I'd say we need to bring Elijah back in." The detective stood.

"You know where to find him," Ryan said.

Detective Kane raised one eyebrow. "I don't understand how that young artist can live on one of the richest estates on the island."

"Mrs. Kim is his sponsor. In return, she gets first pick of his paintings," Shandra said.

The detective pulled out his phone. He walked into the other room talking on it.

"Leilani, you have to think hard. What could you have heard or seen that would have someone terrorizing you? Have you received any threats to keep quiet?"

Her cheeks darkened. "That's what I was looking at on the computer when you arrived at the gallery. Someone had sent me an email through the society's website. It told me if I didn't have a loss of memory about the night Patrick died, I'd be next."

Ryan stepped forward. "Why didn't you tell us that earlier?"

"I didn't want you to think I was trying to take your attention away from the drugs behind the painting. The detective already thinks I killed Patrick. What's to keep him from thinking I've been misleading him and you with all this other stuff that never happens on this island." She sighed. "I moved here because of the low crime rate, my family, and wonderful weather."

Shandra knew Leilani's fiancé had been murdered in the Los Angeles area and the killer never found. She understood her friend's desire to live somewhere that violence of that magnitude wouldn't hurt her again. But it had, and she needed to deal with it.

Detective Kane returned to the room. Ryan immediately filled him in on what they'd just discovered.

"Can you bring that email up on your computer for me?" the detective asked.

"Here, use mine." Shandra grabbed her laptop that was on the side table by the couch. She opened it, put in her passcode, and handed it to Leilani.

While she worked at bringing up the art society website, Shandra mulled over what they'd learned so far tonight. It was a lot, considering the fact the violence against Leilani had escalated.

"Here it is." Her friend spun the computer around so they could all three see the email.

"Who did it come from?" Detective Kane asked.

"I don't know. They had to have found this email through the art society website. I've never heard of this email address." Leilani leaned back on the couch. "I've been thinking and thinking. I don't know what they want me to keep my mouth shut about. I talked to Patrick, saw him fall, and tried to save him. I didn't see anyone…" She stopped. "There was a car."

"Where?" Ryan and Detective Kane said at the same time.

"On the point road as I drove in to see Patrick. It was on the way out." She shook her head. "But Patrick was alive, when I arrived. I talked to him, watched him walk to the cliffside."

"Can you remember anything about the car?" the detective asked.

"It was dark colored. The lights were on so I didn't see who was in the vehicle." She closed her eyes. "It was missing a taillight. That's the best I can do. Sorry. I don't care what the make of a car is. I look at the lines and color."

"Forensics will be in the workroom for a few more hours. They'll need to print all of you to rule out your prints against what they find." Detective Kane motioned for Ryan to follow him with a bob of his head.

Chapter Twenty-three

Ryan stood out on the front step with the detective. This was looking more and more like Elijah Lee had something to do with the deaths, but he wasn't sure what that had to do with the drugs.

"I'm going to go have a talk with Elijah. I'd invite you along, but I think you should stay here in case anything else happens." The detective leaned down and unstrapped his ankle holster. "Take this. Whoever this is, killed twice. Take my backup piece." He handed the holster and weapon over to Ryan.

"Thanks, I've been feeling a bit naked since the murders happened." Ryan checked the Glock 43—it had ten rounds of nine mil—before strapping it onto his leg. No sense getting the women worried if they saw him carrying a gun into the house.

"Like I said, forensics will be here a while. I want them to find something that will help us put a finger on who is messing with our tranquil island." Kane headed to his unmarked vehicle. "Stay alert."

"I will." Ryan waited for the detective to pull out

of the driveway before he pivoted and headed into the house. He found Shandra in the kitchen. "Where's Leilani?"

"Taking a bath. She's relieved she's finally told us everything, but worried she's dragged us into harm." Shandra handed him a cup of coffee. "I have a feeling you and I aren't going to get much sleep tonight."

He sipped the hot brew and nodded. "Good thing we'd planned to stay here two weeks." He grasped her hand, leading her down the hall to the workroom door.

They stood in the doorway, sipping their drinks and watching the forensics team bag every piece of pottery and vacuum the whole area.

Ryan stopped one of the people as they walked by the doorway. "Did anyone figure out how the intruder came in?"

"There's a window pane in the patio door broken. They reached in, unlocked the door, and that was it. People really need to use security systems." The man continued checking surfaces for prints.

"I guess that means you'll be staying down here where you can keep an eye on that door after everyone leaves," Shandra said, with a sigh.

He grinned. "It's either that or see what I can find in the garage to fix it, but that won't keep someone from breaking another pane to reach in. Leilani can call someone to fix it first thing in the morning and install a security system."

Shandra wrinkled her nose. He knew how she felt about alarm systems, but since they'd had several people gain access to her home, she'd agreed to the system. Her cantankerous employee Crazy Lil just added it to her list of why she didn't like him. He grinned thinking about the woman.

"Have you checked in with Lil lately?" he asked.

"It's too late to do it now," Shandra replied.

"They're three hours ahead of us. It's nearly six in the morning there. You know she's up. Give her a call. It will make you feel better." He kissed the top of her head and sent her back toward the living room.

Once she was out of hearing, he started asking the forensics crew questions. "Can you tell if the intruder was looking for something or just causing damage?"

"From the debris and impact on the walls, I'd say it was an angry intruder. Could be because he didn't find what he was looking for or was mad at the woman who lives here."

That didn't help any. It would be hard for Leilani to tell what might be missing with the team bagging up everything that had been broken.

"Have you found any fingerprints on the broken pieces?"

The female who appeared to be the lead team member stopped and studied him. "This is pottery. The artist's prints will be all over them. We haven't the time to check it all for different prints here."

He sighed. It was obvious they thought he was some inquisitive home owner and not in law enforcement like themselves.

He'd go wait in the living room with Shandra and Leilani until the crew left.

~*~

The soft snuffling in the phone made Shandra chuckle. "Sheba, I miss you, too. We'll be home in six more days, I promise."

Howling started and Lil's gruff voice overrode the

166

forlorn call. "She's been looking for you every day the last couple of days. You aren't usually gone this long."

"I know. But I'm glad we'd planned to stay longer. There's been two artists killed and my friend is somehow connected to all of it." Shandra watched Leilani, dressed in sweats and a baggy T-shirt, enter the room.

"I'm glad to hear everything is fine. I'll check in again soon." She hung up. Afraid she'd tell Ryan to change their tickets to an earlier date. She missed her pony-sized cowardly dog, her gruff employee, her horses, and her studio. Her hands had been itching to work with clay the last couple of days. It was always her best way to think things through.

"Everything good back in Huckleberry?" Leilani asked.

"Yes. I just miss all of my animals and even Lil." She chuckled. "The woman is like a burr under a saddle, but she's honest, dependable, and probably the best friend I have next to Ryan."

Leilani's eyes glistened. "I envy you that. While I have family and we're close, I haven't been able to cultivate a friendship here. I thought I had with Brendan, then he tried to make it sexual when I wasn't thinking of him in that way, at all. That's when Francie's claws came out."

Shandra glanced up from where she'd been scrolling through photos of her animals on her phone. "Francie was jealous of you and Brendan?"

"That's the only thing I could think of when she told me to stop getting in the way of Brendan's plans for the society."

Shandra shook her head. "That wasn't jealousy.

That was greed. Though it could be both. She told me that if Brendan didn't start raising money, he would have to get rid of her. But she'd sounded liked she was ready to move on to some other benefactor."

"I'm surprised he hasn't married someone with money." Shandra studied her friend. "Do you happen to know why he hasn't?"

Leilani appeared puzzled. "I don't think I've ever heard him linked with a woman other than the artists he gave scholarships and Francie."

Shandra grabbed her laptop and opened it up. She went to the local newspaper and typed Brendan Darnell into the search tab.

She scrolled to dates that would have been his teens and twenties. The headline popped out at her, but it was the photo that surprised her the most.

"Who do you think that woman looks like?" she asked, pointing at the screen.

"That's Louise Kim. She's not bad for her age, but she was stunning back then."

"She and Brendan became engaged on this date." She clicked each story with Brendan's name and never did see a wedding happen. He was caught for drunk driving half a dozen times. "I think she dumped him."

Continuing to scan the stories, nothing else came up about a marriage. She typed in Louise Teeter, the name in the engagement story and discovered that about the time Brendan was getting his drunk driving tickets, she married Wesley Kim, the owner of an import export company.

Shandra thought of her visit to the Kim Estate. There had been very little Oriental art. She typed in Wesley Kim and discovered his obituary from five years before.

"Has Mrs. Kim changed how she's been living since her husband's death?" Shandra asked.

Leilani peered at her. "What do you mean?"

"Has she seemed to have less money? I would think she would be Brendan's means of getting out of his predicament if they both still had feelings for one another." She itched to talk to Mrs. Kim.

"As far as I know, she's fine. Her husband was good at what he did. They were well respected on the island. In fact, all the islands." Leilani yawned. "I can't believe I'm tired. With all that has happened, I should be buzzing with nerves."

Ryan walked into the living room. "You can go to bed, both of you. I'll lock up after the forensic team leaves and make sure no one comes in through that door during the night."

"Thank you. I'm glad Shandra agreed to be our juror. Otherwise, I would be in jail for a murder I didn't commit and who knows what else would have happened." Leilani leaned over and hugged Shandra. "Thank you for believing in me."

Ryan watched the woman walk up the stairs and sat on the couch beside Shandra. "What do you think about her all of a sudden spilling everything tonight?"

"The threat and her wrecked studio scared her into telling the truth." Shandra spun her computer toward him. "I discovered some interesting things." She went on to tell him what she'd learned about Darnell, Mrs. Kim, and Francie, Darnell's arm candy.

"How do you think this all fits in?" He studied his wife. "None of them have anything to do with the drugs, which according to your dreams, has to do with the deaths."

Her brow wrinkled. She stared at the computer screen for so long, he thought she might have fallen asleep with her eyes open.

"Go to bed. Maybe your grandmother will come to you and we'll have a clearer idea of everything." Ryan closed the laptop and stood, drawing Shandra up beside him. "Sweet dreams." He kissed her and directed her to the stairs.

She spun around at the bottom. "Lil said everything is fine, but Sheba misses me."

He laughed. "She misses you if you go into the next room. I'm glad everything is fine. Go to bed."

Shandra climbed the stairs. When she was out of sight, he headed back to the workroom. The forensic team had started hauling their evidence and equipment out the kitchen door to the garage.

"Thanks," he said to the team leader.

She smiled. "You might want to do something about that door."

"I plan on it." He checked to make sure the door was locked, even though the pane was broken and followed them out to the garage. He closed the garage door and headed back to the workroom, turning out all the lights. In the workroom, he placed a chair inside the door, facing the patio door. The outside light would highlight anyone trying to return tonight.

Ryan leaned back in the chair and ran through everything they knew and what they'd learned tonight. While Shandra championed her friend, she had to realize Leilani was the common denominator between the murders and the things that had happened to her.

Chapter Twenty-four

Shandra walked along the beach. It was hot and sunny. The waves crashed, washing up onto the sand, warming her toes. She wore a long flowing dress and a wide-brimmed straw hat. Up ahead she recognized the cliff with the wet cave. The cliff that Patrick had fallen from.

People stood on the beach. Hawaiian music filled the air. The mood was happy, carefree. She strained to find Ryan in the crowd. As she walked closer, they parted, allowing her to walk to the front.

The bride and groom faced her.

She screamed.

They were Patrick and Billie. They pointed at her. As if accusing her of killing them.

"I didn't! I didn't!"

"Shandra, wake up. Shandra." Hands shook her shoulders.

Her eyelids fluttered open. She stared into Ryan's

brown, concerned eyes. Shandra wrapped her arms around him and held onto his warmth, breathing in his scent. He was safety.

"What was the dream about?" he asked, holding her close, allowing her time to press the fear down and analyze what she'd dreamed.

"I was back at the wet cave. There was a wedding on the beach. I looked for you, but you weren't there. Then the bride and groom turned around. It was Patrick and Billie, pointing at me. Accusing me." She shoved away from Ryan. "My coming here messed everything up. Whatever was going down, would have, if I hadn't been asked to juror by Leilani."

"Go to sleep. We'll ask her who the board had picked before she said you were judging." Ryan settled her back down on the bed.

"What time is it?"

"Four. I heard your scream." He twisted, peering at the door. "Why didn't Leilani come see what happened?"

Ryan headed for the door.

Shandra jumped out of bed, still trying to gather her bearings but hurrying behind him.

At the bedroom door, Ryan knocked. "Leilani?"

Shandra pushed by him, turned the doorknob, and shoved the door open. The bed was empty. She hurried to the bathroom. It was empty as well. "She's not here." Shandra spun to her husband. "Do you think someone came in and kidnapped her?"

Ryan shook his head. "She snuck out."

Shandra wobbled over to the bed and sunk down onto it. "Why? We'd ruled her out of having killed anyone."

"My guess is, talking about everything triggered a memory that she went to check out." Ryan pulled Shandra to her feet. "Do you want to go back to bed?"

"No. I won't be able to sleep wondering where she went and what she said that sent her off in the middle of the night." Shandra shoved her hair off her face and stared at Ryan. "If I crank coffee, I could use some now."

"How about a strong cup of tea?" Ryan led her out of the bedroom and down the stairs.

When they sat in the kitchen at the island sipping their drinks—coffee for Ryan, tea for her, Shandra stood.

Ryan grasped her hand. "Where are you going?"

"To get my laptop and sketch pad. We have to figure out where she went. She could be in danger."

Ryan released her.

She wandered into the living room and realized her phone was missing. "She took it!"

"Took what?" Ryan appeared in the living room doorway.

"My phone. Why would she take my phone? You have yours. We can call her with it." Shandra picked up her laptop, sketch pad, and pencil. Why take her phone? Did it have to do with photos she took?

"Try calling her phone," Shandra said as they sat down back at the island and she opened her laptop. She went straight to photos downloaded. "She must have taken my phone because of a photo I took."

The Hawaiian song that played when Leilani's phone rang could be faintly heard upstairs.

"She didn't take her phone, but took yours." Ryan was already scrolling. He hit a button and listened.

"Your phone is going straight to voicemail."

"Why take mine if she didn't want to be contacted?" Shandra pulled up the photos she'd taken so far. There weren't many as they had done little sightseeing.

"The only thing I can think of are the photos of Patrick's painting. She sent those to me via email." She opened up the folder with the photos.

"She would need your password to get into the email." Ryan peered over her shoulder. He had a hand on the counter on each side of the laptop.

"Not necessarily. It is set to always open." She stared at the painting photo. There had to be something in the painting that they'd missed.

They both jumped as Ryan's phone buzzed. He straightened, then walked into the living room.

Ryan didn't want Shandra to hear the conversation. "Detective, we were getting ready to call you."

"Has someone tried to get back in the house?"

"No, the owner is missing. It looks like Leilani remembered something and went to confront someone. She took Shandra's phone." As soon as the words came out, he realized why she took the phone.

"Why would she take the phone?"

"So we could track her. She must have realized I'd have GPS tracking on Shandra's phone." He headed back into the kitchen. Shandra hunched over the laptop, staring at an enlarged version of the hideous painting that started all of this.

"What did you call about?" Ryan asked, motioning for Shandra to move out of the way.

She refused, shaking her head and pointing at the screen.

"To tell you that Elijah Lee is at the station and lawyering up."

"Let me guess. Mrs. Kim is providing his lawyer." Ryan had a feeling when they first met the woman, she had too much of an interest in the young man, more than liking his painting.

"You got it. Let me know when you pinpoint Ms. Brown's location." He hung up.

"We need to track your phone," Ryan said, again trying to take the computer from his wife.

"Wait."

He glanced over to her right hand. She was drawing something. "What do you see?"

"Numbers. Maybe. It's really faint." She continued and finally leaned back. "What do you make of them?"

Ryan stared at the numbers. "Were they all smashed together or some distance between some."

"Just like that."

He shrugged. "I don't know what they could be. I'm pulling up your phone on the tracking app." He put in the passwords and soon had a map of Kaua'i on the screen. "She left here at three, so she's not that far ahead of us."

"Where is she now?" Shandra asked, writing the numbers out in different patterns.

"She's almost to Hanalei."

Before he could register the significance, Shandra said, "She's going to see Saul." She glanced up. "Why Saul?"

He shook his head. "Darnell lives up there, too."

"She wouldn't go see Brendan. She doesn't like him…" she trailed off. "She may be going to see Francie. What was it she said about her?" Shandra shoved the sketch pad with the numbers to the center of the island.

"She said Francie's claws came out when Leilani wouldn't let Brendan make the art society for profit. And Francie told me if Brendan didn't start making money, she was going to be kicked out." Shandra stood. "I'm getting dressed. We need to make sure nothing happens to Leilani. And I want to talk to Brendan."

Chapter Twenty-five

Following the cell phone's GPS, Ryan drove over the speed limit, hoping Detective Kane would vouch for him if he was pulled over. Ryan parked behind Leilani's car in the driveway of Brendan Darnell's Estate. There were lights on in the downstairs rooms facing the driveway. It was 6 AM and if there were still servants, he was sure they were the ones who had switched on all the lights when Leilani arrived.

"I hope nothing has happened to Leilani," Shandra said, as they walked hand-in-hand up to the massive door.

"They would be stupid to do anything to her with what has happened." Ryan hoped this appeased his wife. He rapped the large pineapple shaped iron door knocker.

The door opened.

"You're not the police," a woman in her sixties said with disapproval.

"We're here to talk with Mr. Darnell, Francie, and Ms. Brown," Ryan said.

"I called the police to take away Ms. Brown. She's been ranting about needing to talk to Mr. Darnell. He doesn't like to be disturbed until nine."

Ryan pushed by the woman, leading Shandra behind him. "Where's Ms. Brown? And wake up Mr. Darnell, or I will."

The woman huffed. "You'll find the woman in the dining room, that way." She pointed to a hall to the right.

Ryan strode down the hall until he spotted a room with a light on. Stepping inside, they found Leilani tied to a chair with a gag in her mouth.

Shandra ran over to the chair and pulled the gag out of her friend's mouth before untying her. "What happened?"

"I knocked on the door, asked to see Brendan, and the housekeeper brought me in here. Someone knocked me on the head, and I woke up tied to the chair." Leilani's pupils were dilated.

"Whoever hit you did a good job. I think you have a concussion." Ryan put a hand on the woman's shoulder as she started to rise. "Stay put until we talk to Darnell. I sent the housekeeper to get him."

While they waited, Ryan texted Kane that they were at Brendan Darnell's house and Ms. Brown had been attacked. He figured that would get the police here faster than the housekeeper's call. If she'd made it. It was highly unlikely she'd called the cops. Not after attacking a person and tying them up.

Fifteen, then twenty minutes, passed. "I'm going to go look for them. You two stay here." Ryan pulled the weapon from the ankle holster.

"Be careful," Shandra said, from the chair she'd placed beside Leilani's.

He sent her a smile and slipped out of the room. Most large houses with staff had a back staircase. That was the one he'd take to the second floor. He found it in the hallway outside the kitchen. He checked that room first. There was coffee brewing and the scent of a sweet roll baking.

On the staircase, he moved with caution, listening to anyone above or below him. At the top, he followed the faint glow of light under a door.

At the door, he placed an ear to the crack and listened. Nothing.

He put his hand on the handle, pushed down, and the door opened.

Brendan Darnell was a large lump in the massive bed at the far side of the room. A lamp near the door was the reason for the light underneath.

Ryan knocked loudly on the open door.

"Huh? What? Who's there?" Darnell raised up in bed, his thinning hair was tousled, and his dark blue pajama top wrinkled.

"Mr. Darnell, it's Ryan Greer, Shandra Higheagle's husband. We need to talk."

The man glanced at the clock beside his bed. "It's six-thirty. Come back at ten." He started to lie back down and then stopped. "Where's my housekeeper? How did you get by her?"

"She seems to have disappeared after bashing Ms. Brown on the head and tying her up." Ryan strode across the room. "I suggest you get some clothes on and come down. I've called the police."

Darnell's scowl slacked and his face paled. "Why would you do that?"

"Because your housekeeper struck and detained a woman. A woman who came here to talk to you." Ryan grabbed the clothes draped over a chair. He tossed them at the man. "Put these on and come down to the dining room."

He left the room, leaving the door open. Using the back stairs, he popped into the kitchen, and placed a cup of water in the microwave. While it was heating, Ryan set the brewed coffee on a tray next to the coffeemaker that already had three cups, sugar and cream. He found tea bags, added them to the tray, added the cup of hot water, and last placed the baked sweet rolls on the tray.

Shandra glanced up as Ryan entered the room. "Is that where you've been. Baking and setting up a tray?" She smiled as he shook his head.

"I woke Darnell up first. Saw that this was ready and grabbed it on my way by the kitchen." He placed the tray on the table near she and Leilani. "I didn't see any sign of the housekeeper or Francie."

Shandra put a tea bag in the hot water and handed Leilani a cup of coffee that Ryan had poured. "Leilani came here to talk to Brendan. After I showed her the photo of Brendan and Mrs. Kim having been engaged, she started thinking about how the two treated one another at the meetings."

Leilani nodded. "At first they were cold to one another. I didn't understand, and no one who knew them both said anything."

"What made you want to talk to Darnell all of a sudden?" Ryan asked.

"When Brendan first started talking about dropping the non-profit for the art society, Mrs. Kim told him to talk to her after the meeting. Then they seemed to be on better terms, until she moved Elijah into the pool house at her estate. After that, they were back to staring daggers at each other. And Francie became more vicious with her comments of everyone on the society board." Leilani sighed and rubbed her head. "I just wanted to understand what was going on."

"It could have waited until morning, and you could have brought one of us with you," Ryan said.

Shandra nodded. "I told her that. For some reason she felt compelled to come that very minute. Probably the adrenaline from having been victimized."

Leilani's eyes widened. "You mean I wasn't thinking clear because of my work being destroyed?"

"What do you think?" Shandra peered into her friend's eyes and saw confusion.

"Ever since the night of Patrick's death, I don't know what to think or do."

Shandra put an arm around Leilani's shoulders. "I know."

The rap of the brass knocker echoed down the hall.

"I'll get that. It's bound to be Kane." Ryan disappeared out into the hall.

The sound of voices murmured in the hall and entered the room. It was Detective Kane, Brendan, and Ryan.

"I don't understand why you had to call in the—" Brendan stopped when his gaze landed on Leilani. He hurried across the room. "I'm so sorry. Ryan said my housekeeper hit you on the head and tied you up."

Shandra shook her head. "Your housekeeper was in

front of her. Someone else hit her from behind. Hard. Look at this lump." She ran a hand over the growing lump on the back of Leilani's head.

Detective Kane moved closer to look. He pulled out his phone. "Officer Miller, come in here and escort Ms. Brown to the emergency room." Directing his attention to Leilani, he said, "I'll have an officer take you to be looked at and stay with you until I come get your statement."

"I don't need." She winced. "Okay, I'll go. But you have to know, I only came here to ask Brendan some questions. I didn't come here to harm anyone."

"I know the questions," Shandra added, glancing at Brendan who peered at the door as if he wanted to be somewhere else.

Officer Miller entered the dining room. Shandra was glad to see the person escorting Leilani was female. That would make her friend feel more comfortable.

The two left and Detective Kane faced Brendan. "Have a seat."

When the owner of the estate was seated, the detective asked, "Where is your housekeeper?"

"She should be in the kitchen making my breakfast."

"She's not," Ryan said, sitting on the other side of Brendan.

Shandra sat across from him. "Where's Francie?"

He scowled. "I would assume in her room if he," Brendan pointed to Ryan, "hasn't barged in to wake her up."

Detective Kane raised an eyebrow. "Where is her room?"

"Up the main stairs, go left, and third room on the

left." Brendan reached for a cup of coffee.

Shandra sighed. She wanted to ask Brendan questions, but it was obvious, as the only woman present, she should go see if Francie had been sleeping through all of this. "I'll go see if she's in her bed."

"Be careful," Ryan said.

She smiled. "Always."

He laughed and she walked down the hall followed by what she was pretty sure was Ryan telling the detective how she never follows orders.

She climbed the stairs, turned left, counted the doors, and knocked on the third door on the left. Nothing.

She knocked louder.

Still nothing.

She grasped the latch and opened the door. Darkness was her first impression. Empty was her second.

Feeling along the wall inside the door, her hand connected with a light switch. She flicked it on and blinked, getting her eyes accustomed to the light. The bed was unmade. Drawers were pulled out as if someone had hastily grabbed clothing out. She walked deeper into the room and spotted the door to the large closet open. On a shelf an obvious gap showed where a suitcase was missing. The woman had fled. But why and where?

Shandra pivoted, strode across the room, and down the stairs as quickly as she could. Stopping at the dining room door she asked, "Where does the housekeeper stay?"

Brendan looked perplexed before saying, "The room off the kitchen."

Shandra hurried down the hall. The echo of footsteps behind her made her smile. That would be Ryan. She entered the kitchen, stopping long enough to spot the door to the room, standing open.

Ryan stepped up behind her. "What's going on?"

"Francie packed a bag and is gone." She walked into the small sitting room. Crossed the room and found drawers open, the closet door open, and what looked like a hasty get-away. "They both took off. I don't know if it's because they had something to do with the deaths or because they would be in trouble for what they did to Leilani."

"Let's go have a discussion with Darnell," Ryan said, grasping her hand and leading her back down the hall to the dining room.

The detective's gaze landed on her.

"They're both gone," Shandra said.

"Gone? You mean dead?" Brendan's face puckered up. "Oh God, what have I done?"

Chapter Twenty-six

"What have you done?" Ryan asked, wondering who the man thought killed the two women.

"I shouldn't have listened to Francie. She insisted I push to get the society for profit. She said we could use it to launder money. I was desperate. I can't lose this home, too. I'd be a laughing stock. I'd be dumped from all the social events." Darnell gulped his coffee.

"Did you kill the two women?" Detective Kane asked, it was apparent he'd figured out the women had fled and weren't dead, but was toying with the man who seemed ready to spill everything.

The man's face paled even more. His mouth opened as his eyelids blinked uncontrollably. "No! No, I didn't kill them. I was asleep. I didn't hear a thing."

"Then tell us who killed them," Ryan said, wishing they had thought to record this. Neither he nor Kane had pulled anything out to write it all down.

"It had to be Saul. That's who Francie got the idea

from. She's been banging him for over a year and learning all about illegal ways to make money." He nodded and his complexion darkened. "It had to be that scum of the earth." Darnell pointed to Shandra. "You should have never allowed his paintings in the exhibition. He doesn't deserve any recognition."

Ryan jumped in. "She only looked at the work, she didn't know anything about any of the artist's backgrounds. Like Patrick and Billie. Can you explain their deaths?"

Darnell stared at him. "What do they have to do with Francie and her mother?"

"Her mother?" Shandra spoke up.

"My housekeeper is Francie's mother. The old bat wanted me to marry her daughter until she realized I was losing everything." He narrowed his eyes. "Talk about two gold-diggers. Those two are the biggest. Francie ran into trouble with the law on the mainland and her mom suggested she'd make a nice addition to my life. That was an even bigger mistake than… Never mind."

"Than letting Louise Teeter marry Welsey Kim?" Shandra asked. She was tired of waiting to ask her questions. It was obvious that the man hadn't a clue where the two women had gone. What she didn't understand was why they felt the need to knock out Leilani when she'd arrived?

Brendan's head whipped around, and he stared at her. "How did you know?"

"I browsed the newspaper archives trying to figure out what reason you may have had for being the playboy when you really weren't." She studied him.

His defenses sloughed off and he shook his head.

"Someone told Louise they'd seen me with one of her friends. A friend from a wealthier family. She wouldn't listen. I'd been asking her friend what I should get Louise for a wedding gift. But she's always flown off the handle, only that time it was like twice as bad. We both said things. I know I said things I regretted half an hour later. When I went to her house to apologize, I wasn't let in. Then I heard she'd booked a flight for the mainland. She lived there for over a year. When she came back, she was engaged to Wesley. I tried to talk to her again, but I'd been drinking a lot after she left. She said it was a good thing she'd found out all of my weaknesses before she married me."

Shandra had to know. "After Wesley died, did you try to get back with her?"

He shook his head. "I knew it was a lost cause. Then about a year ago, she contacted me. Tried to tell me some story that we had a son together."

Shandra quickly did the math with the dates she knew and the age of a certain artist. She decided to ease into it. "Did you and Louise sleep together before she called off the wedding?"

An innocent, sweet smile tipped his lips. She could almost see the young man Mrs. Lee fell in love with.

"We did. But I had protection. I know if she did have a child, it wasn't mine." He uttered the last sentence as if half convincing himself.

"You do know that condoms back then were only about eighty percent effective?" Ryan jumped in.

Shandra wondered at how he was so adamant about the percentage. Did he have a child he hadn't told her about? Shaking that off, she returned her attention to Brendan.

"Think about it. You yourself said she was even more emotional and wouldn't listen to your side when she thought you were fooling around with her friend. She left right away and didn't come back for a year."

"What does all of this have to do with my two homicides and Ms. Brown being attacked?" Detective Kane asked.

"I'm thinking nothing," Ryan said.

Shandra shook her head. "I don't know, but Mrs. Kim wanted to have Brendan believe they had a child together. What do you have that she would want to be in the hands of your child?" She hadn't noticed any art that stood out as worth a lot of money. He had admitted he'd been selling off land around the island to cover his costs and continue living normally.

The man appeared completely deflated. He shook his head, staring at his hands clasped in front of him on the table. "She never—" His head raised and he peered into her face. "Patrick's studio, the cliff. I own it."

Detective Kane spun his chair and faced the man. "I looked it up. It is/was owned by Patrick James."

Brendan shook his head. "I signed it over to him to change the legal name on the land so it couldn't be taken away from me, but then he signed a document that gave the land back to me when he left the island, married, or died…" He glanced at each one of them. "I swear, I didn't kill him. I wanted that land to not be tied to me so it wouldn't get taken away."

"Why would James agree to this?" Ryan asked.

Shandra was thinking the same thing. Had he become greedy and decided he wanted to keep the land and told Brendan he wouldn't leave or get married so the land would always belong to him?

"He knew he'd never make enough money selling his paintings to have a place to live. He liked the cliff, the solitude, and even though I said he turned me down for the scholarship, I only said that because he was living on my land, but I didn't want anyone to find out." Brendan raised his empty glass to his lips and set it down.

Shandra refilled his cup. "Why would Mrs. Kim want that cliff?"

"To set up her boy-toy Elijah, I'd say." Brendan spit out the name with venom.

She wondered if she should tell him that boy-toy could be their son? No, not yet. Let that come out later.

Ryan's phone buzzed. He frowned then handed the phone to Shandra.

She understood his frown. He probably had to remember why her phone number would pop up when she was in the same room.

"Hello?"

"It's Leilani. Do you know how much longer Detective Kane will be? They said, as long as I have someone to look after me, I can get out of here."

"Just a minute." She focused on the detective. "Leilani is ready to leave the hospital and wanted to know how much longer she should wait for you."

He stood. "Tell her I'll be there in twenty minutes and I'll take her home."

Shandra hid the smile fluttering at her lips. It seemed the detective was getting personal with her friend. "He said, he'll be there in twenty and will take you home. We should be there by then too."

"Thank you."

Shandra ended the call, watching the detective

walk out of the room.

Ryan's phone buzzed in her hand. Jenny. She handed the phone to Ryan.

He stepped out of the room to take the call.

"I think you're going to need to figure out a better way to keep your family's legacy than hiding property under other people's names and trying to make the art society a place to launder money."

Brendan nodded. "It all went against my principals, but I felt as if I was against a wall. I don't understand where my money went. My accountant assured me that I have just over spent and with the state of interests and stocks, my assets are declining."

"I think you need to find a new accountant to look over your books." Shandra stood as Ryan walked into the room.

"We need to go. Jenny has someone for us to meet." Ryan took her hand and led her out of the house and to the rental car.

"Who are we going to see now?"

"The young man who was dealing at the bar the other night."

Chapter Twenty-seven

Ryan grinned as they drove up to the fruit and drink stand where they'd met the man who told them the tales of treasures and little people. He had a feeling the man was one of Jenny's informants from her police days.

Jenny sat on a stool with the scar-headed kid from the bar next to her. When the kid saw Ryan, he stood. The stool fell over and his arm stretched out, stopping him. Jenny had him handcuffed to the bar.

"Jenny," Ryan sat on the other side of the kid and Shandra sat on the other side of him.

"This is Tarzan," Jenny said by way of introductions.

Shandra made a slight snort sound as if holding in a laugh. Ryan had to give her credit she didn't know anything about who this guy was, but she was keeping her ears open.

The thin old man, Sam, placed drinks in front of

them. "Enjoy," he said, before disappearing out the back of the hut.

"Tarzan, we saw you give a young blonde woman at the Kauai Luau Bar a packet of Ice. She gave it to me." Ryan glanced at Jenny. He didn't know what to say. They hadn't been able to compare it with the drugs found in the cave. But the timeline for this guy selling fit with everything else.

"And I took it to the HIDTA and they compared it to other Ice that had been confiscated and guess what?" Jenny sipped her drink and waited.

The man squirmed but didn't say anything.

"It wasn't part of a shipment that was confiscated from the Phang dealers. Which means, you can cooperate with us and the police, or I'll turn you over to Phang." She smiled and wagged a finger between her and Ryan. "We had a discussion with Phang about this Ice, and he is very interested in learning who is crowding into his territory."

Tarzan was sweating now. And it wasn't from being hot. The large droplets of perspiration trickling from his forehead were from fear. Ryan even knew the smell. He'd witnessed it in the military and working undercover with gangs in Chicago.

"Who are you dealing for?" Ryan asked. "You tell us, and we won't tell Phang."

"You don't understand. I'm dead either way." The young man didn't evoke the bravado he had at the bar the other night. He was scared.

"The police can protect you," Jenny said.

"Like they protected those two artists?" Tarzan glared at Jenny. His attention was on her.

"What about the artists?" Shandra said from the

other side of Ryan.

"You don't even know about them? How are you going to help me?" He shouted and tried to get away again. This time yanking on his arm like a desperate animal.

"Calm down. We know about the artists. But how are they mixed up in this?" Ryan asked, grabbing him by the arm and sitting him down.

"I'm not sure what they did, but they were mixed up in it getting to the island. Since they died, the supply has dropped off."

Someone on the beach laughed loudly.

Tarzan flinched and swiveled his head to study the sand and ocean beyond. "They know I'm talking to you, I'll be dead soon."

"We'll see that you survive." Jenny pulled out her phone and walked away from the shack, talking.

"Did you know the artists who died?" Shandra asked.

Tarzan studied her. "You don't look like a cop."

"I'm not. I am an artist."

Ryan leaned back so Shandra could use her touch at getting information out of people. He'd learned when they first met, she had a way of making people comfortable enough to talk to her.

"You knew them?" Tarzan asked.

"Yeah." She didn't elaborate.

"I knew Billie. She and Elijah, her boyfriend, would come to one of the bars I frequent." He shook his head. "She didn't need to die. She knew how to keep her mouth shut."

"What did she know?" Shandra asked.

His eyes widened. Fear, again. "I don't know."

Ryan knew that was a lie, but he kept quiet as Jenny returned.

"If you two want to head out, I'll wait for someone to come pick Tarzan up." She said the name with as much sarcasm as Ryan had ever heard a word uttered.

"I think it would be best if we stay with you. More eyes to keep watch," Ryan said.

"Nothing to worry about," Sam said, stepping into the shack. "We'll keep him in here until backup arrives."

Ryan grinned. It appeared not only was Sam an informant, he was also a retired policeman. "Works for me. Let me know if you learn anything else."

"I will." Jenny unlatched the cuff on the bar and led Tarzan into the back of the building.

"I bet Leilani and Detective Kane are waiting for us to arrive so he can leave," Shandra said.

"I'm sure the detective doesn't mind waiting." Ryan had noticed the vibe going on between the two. Even when Kane was certain Leilani had something to do with Patrick's death.

Chapter Twenty-eight

Detective Kane opened the door when they arrived. "I thought you were right behind me?"

Shandra smiled. "We had a detour. How's Leilani?"

"She's in the living room staring at the wall. She's not to watch TV, or use any devices for twenty-four hours. She refused to lay down. Said she had to talk to you when you got here." He motioned for Ryan to follow him out the door.

Shandra walked into the living room. Leilani had a cold drink on the side table next to her and a magazine on her lap.

"I thought you'd never get here. I want to apologize for running out like I did and taking your phone." She smiled sheepishly. "But you knew where to find me."

"Why did you think you needed to confront Brendan in the wee hours of the morning?" Shandra settled on the couch next to her friend.

"I figured out Elijah is probably his and Louise Kim's son." Her eyes sparkled with excitement.

"And how did you come up with that?" Shandra said, hoping there wasn't any inflection in her voice.

"The same way you did. The dates of how the engagement happened, then she left, and came back and married. I wanted to know if he knew Elijah was his son and if that was why he was so desperate to get more money. To buy Elijah's love from his mother." She shrugged. "You have to admit, it would make a great movie."

"Or soap opera," Shandra muttered. "That still doesn't tell me why you wanted to see him when most people were sleeping." It clicked. "Ahhh, you didn't want Francie to hear you talking."

"Yes. She'd just go dig her claws into the younger Darnell." Leilani made a face.

"You're right to have been skeptical of Francie, but I don't think Brendan would have believed you." The way the man had denied it earlier, made Shandra wonder if he were sterile. That would be the only way he could be certain. Especially, since he'd admitted to their having sex.

"Do you know why Mr. and Mrs. Kim never had children?" Shandra asked.

Leilani shook her head. "I never thought about it. Maybe because all of his business dealings weren't legal?"

Shandra jumped on that. "What do you mean?"

"If you look up Kim Imports in the newspaper archives, you'll see it was subpoenaed several times over the years to present records. They always seemed to pass whatever the courts were looking for, but word on the island is he didn't deal in only legal merchandise."

"Was one of the illegal products drugs?"

"At one time the company was linked to the opium coming onto the island. It was stopped by police and there wasn't any more mention of it. That's also when Wesley took over the import company from his father." Leilani yawned. "I didn't get any sleep last night."

"You can go up to your room," Shandra offered as Ryan walked in the living room.

"No. I want to know what's going on. Ike said he'd tell me everything when this is over."

"Ike?" Shandra asked.

Leilani blushed. "Detective Kane. He said he now realizes I am telling the truth." Her cheeks darkened even more. "He hinted that we might see one another after the case is solved."

"That's good. Unless you think you aren't ready to date someone who could be in danger?" Shandra studied her friend.

"I told you. I came here because the crime rate is very low on this island. These two murders are an anomaly." Leilani rose.

"I'll check on you in a few hours." Shandra said, patting the couch next to her for Ryan to sit.

Leilani waved a hand in the air and climbed the stairs.

"What did Ike, Detective Kane, want to talk to you about?" she asked.

"Francie and her mom were picked up at the airport trying to buy a ticket to the mainland. He had them hauled to the station for questioning." Ryan's gaze flicked to the stairs. "Leilani tell you why she stole out of here in the middle of the night?"

"Early morning," she corrected him. "She wanted to talk to Brendan without Francie around."

"She didn't trust her? Why?"

"Something about getting her claws into Elijah if, as she believed, he is the son of Brendan and Louise Kim."

Ryan shook his head. "I don't know. That seems a bit risky for Mrs. Kim to allow her illegitimate son to live at her estate. I would think more people would put it together, unless she planned to go public with the information."

"I thought the pride she showed when telling us about the painting seemed more than one who was helping a buddying artist." Shandra glanced at her watch. "Want to grab something to eat?"

"We can get something here, so we can keep an eye on Leilani. Kane is worried she'll do something foolish like this morning."

Shandra knew she should stay here with her friend, but they had so many possibilities and loose ends, she felt the need to talk with more people. "Have you heard from Jenny. Is Tarzan, what a goofy name for a drug dealer, talking yet?"

"I told Kane about him and she called while I was with him. So far, our surfer is keeping his mouth sealed shut. Whoever is the head of the drug smuggling, he is more afraid of them than Phang." Ryan stood and held out a hand. "Come on. Let's make—"

The doorbell rang.

Ryan answered it.

A big burly man with sandals, board shorts, a

button-up Hawaiian print shirt and tool box stood in the doorway. "Ike called and said this house needs a security system." He glanced over his shoulder. "I brought my cousin to fix the broken window." A thinner version of the man at the door walked up with something wrapped in a twelve-by-twelve bubble wrap and his own toolbox.

"Come in. He said you'd be showing up." Ryan led the two men to the workroom and Shandra entered the kitchen.

By the time she had bread, lunch meat, and vegetables set out, Ryan returned to the room.

"That's why you really didn't want to leave, isn't it?" she said, making a sandwich.

"That and I promised Kane I wouldn't leave Leilani alone. If it wasn't Francie who broke in here, then there is still someone out there that is trying to scare Leilani." Ryan made his sandwich.

They sat down at the counter in the kitchen to eat. It was farther from the workroom than the dining or living rooms and Ryan sat where he could see the front door.

"Do you think the person who was leaving the cliff the night Patrick died thinks Leilani knew who they were?" Shandra had been wondering how they could figure out who it could have been.

"That's possible. Or they think she picked up something at the studio." Ryan put his sandwich down. "Did she say if she picked anything up? Did she see the painting?"

"I don't know. She didn't say." Shandra looked at her watch. "I'll ask her in a couple of hours when I check on her. Right now, she's probably dead to the world and wouldn't be able to think straight."

The thought of Leilani seeing something at the studio nagged at Shandra. "Can you ask Detective Kane to send us the crime scene photos from the studio?" She paused. "And the statements from Saul's neighbors after Billie's death."

Ryan studied his wife. He didn't have a clue what she was thinking, but that usually meant she was piecing things together in her abstract way. "I'll give him a call. Out front. He might have called these guys to work on the house, but at this point it's hard to trust anyone."

He walked out the front door and stood in the shade of a banana tree and called the detective. The call went to his voicemail. He was probably questioning either Tarzan, Francie, or her mom. Ryan left his requests and ended the call as Jenny pulled in behind the rental car.

She scanned the van the workers came in. "Friends of Leilani's?"

"I don't know. They said Detective Kane sent them here to install a security system and fix her door."

"Why? What happened?" She shoved by him and into the house.

That's when he realized they hadn't had time to tell her about the break-in or her cousin's blow to the head.

"Leilani?" Jenny shouted.

Shandra ran out of the kitchen. "Shhh. She's resting."

"What happened? Why didn't you tell me earlier?" Jenny glared at Shandra.

Ryan stepped between them. "Sorry. We knew she was in good hands. Things have been happening so fast since last night, we can't keep up with who knows what."

They led her into the kitchen and told her about the break-in, Leilani's early morning trip, and subsequent knot on the head.

Shandra smiled. "She and Detective Kane are becoming friends."

"Really. Now that's news. I didn't think she'd ever take up with a cop after what happened in L.A." Jenny picked up the iced tea Shandra poured for her.

"Me either."

"Care to enlighten me?" Ryan asked, wondering what the art show chair's past held that would make her leery of a cop.

"She lost her fiancé to violence. Cops could never find out who killed him. That's why she left the mainland and landed here, where the violence is usually kept to drunken brawls or marital spats." Jenny studied Ryan. "You hear anything about what Tarzan had to say?"

"The last I talked to Kane, he'd clammed up." Ryan sipped his tea. Then set it down. "Phang wouldn't happen to know more than he told us the other day?"

She chuckled. "He probably does. But I honestly think he was just curious about what we knew. That was the only reason he talked with us."

Ryan's phone dinged. He glanced at the message. *I sent what you requested to Shandra's email.*

Chapter Twenty-nine

The two men left ten minutes after Ryan received the text from the detective.

Shandra sat on the couch and opened her computer. She clicked on the email marked photos, first. "I'm glad Detective Kane was willing to let us look at these." She started with the first photo. Ryan and Jenny sat on either side of her, staring at the screen. "When we find something of interest, we'll wake Leilani and ask her about it."

She slowly scrolled from photo to photo. "Is it just me or does this room look as if someone had been looking for something?"

"I agree," Jenny said.

"Something small, like the search of Billie's house and Leilani's workroom." Ryan leaned back. "Whatever it was, they believe Leilani has it."

"I'll go wake her and bring her down." Jenny crossed to the entry and the stairs, disappearing to the second floor.

Shandra continued to study the photos. "Where is the painting? Who took it? Was it because of the numbers I found?" She glanced up, grabbed her sketch book with the numbers, and studied them.

"Let me look over the interviews at the second homicide." Ryan took the computer from Shandra and clicked out of the photos and into the email with the interviews.

Shandra continued to study the numbers, grouping them like phone numbers. Three, three, four. But she ended up with two extra numbers. She sectioned them into four digits, five digits, and so on.

Jenny and Leilani entered the room.

"Leilani, when you were in Patrick's studio did things look out of place?" Shandra asked.

"No. Nothing other than his usual mess. Paint spatters, paint stained rags on the floor by his easel. That kind of thing." She sat down and Jenny continued down the hall.

"Did he give you anything that night? Ask you to hold anything?" Ryan asked, glancing up from the interviews he'd been reading.

She shook her head slightly. "No. He didn't give me anything. But a few seconds after he stormed out of the studio, it sounded like a car door closed." She closed her eyes. "But my car was the only one there."

Ryan shoved the computer into Shandra's lap and left the room.

Jenny walked into the living room, carrying an iced tea that she handed to Leilani. "Where's he going?"

"To look through Leilani's car." Shandra understood that whatever the people were looking for could have been in her friend's car all along. That is if someone hadn't already looked through it.

She caught Jenny up to speed on the numbers she found on the painting, and the fact someone had been looking for something smaller than a painting.

"Can you remember anything about the car or driver you saw besides the fact it only had one taillight?" Shandra asked. She needed to stay focused on the questions, but her thoughts were out in the car with Ryan, willing him to find something to help them clear all of this up.

"You saw a car with one taillight at the point the night the guy died?" Jenny questioned her cousin.

"Yeah. It was going out as I came in." Leilani stared at Jenny. "Why?"

"Sam said there's been a car meeting with Tarzan once a week that is missing a taillight. He said it had different plates every time. When he turned the plates in, they were from a stolen car." Jenny stared at the numbers on the sketch pad.

"I would say that means Patrick was tangled up with the new drug smugglers on the island." Shandra glanced up as Ryan came in holding a small blue sketch book by the corner with a candy wrapper.

"Does this belong to you?" he asked

"The candy wrapper, yes. The book, no. Where did you find it?" Leilani sat forward.

"Under the rubber mat in the back seat of your car." Ryan grabbed two tissues from a box and used them to not touch the book while he opened it.

"It has numbers, too." Shandra said.

"But look at the top of the page." Jenny pointed at the letters. They were: D, TL, TH.

"The first two numbers never go past thirty. They could be days of the month?" Shandra said. "That would mean the D is for day or date."

"TL and TH, what do you make of that?" Ryan asked Jenny.

"They are four numbers. The first two never go higher than twenty-four and the second ones go to fifty-nine. They must be times."

"Tide low and tide high!" Leilani exclaimed. "I was trying to get to a beach a month or so ago at low tide to see what it looked like for a project I was working on." Her smile melted. "That project and many others are gone now."

"But *you* are safe," Shandra reminded her.

"That's true. I'm alive and can make more art. Poor Billie and Patrick will never share their gifts again." Tears glistened in her friend's eyes.

"We'll need to see a tide chart and compare the times to the high and low to figure out where these tides were for." Ryan pulled out his phone.

"We know where the tides were for," Shandra said. "Halekoa Point. He got the information for the high and low tides to whoever was dropping off the drugs and to whoever was picking them up in the cave we found."

"He must have said something about having the information written down to the person leaving with the one taillight when Leilani arrived," Jenny said. "They must have turned around and ransacked the place while she was trying to save Patrick."

"Did you go back in the studio after trying to help him?" Shandra asked.

"No. I walked to my car, started it, and left." Leilani stared at the book. "Is that why someone ruined my workroom?"

"I think so. I'm calling Detective Kane and letting him know what we found." Ryan stepped out of the room.

"Now we need to find the car with one taillight," Shandra said.

"I think I know how to find the car." Jenny grinned. "Look at the last numbers on this list."

Chapter Thirty

"Do you really think they'll go through with a drop-off and pick-up after we found the cave?" Shandra asked as she, Ryan, and Detective Kane stood in the shadows of the trees closest to the beach and wet cave at Halekoa Point.

"They don't know that we found the cave. The chest you found was gone by the time our divers went in to get it." Detective Kane held binoculars to his eyes.

"But they have to know you have Tarzan locked up," she countered. While it made sense to see who dropped off the drugs and have the Coast Guard pick them up and then wait for the island part of the operation to show up, she had an uneasy feeling they wouldn't learn anything from this. The wedding in her dream had been on this beach. The dead couple had pointed at her.

She should know the answer to this without sitting here for hours waiting for someone to show.

Grandmother had sat on that rock and pointed… to

the shore. No, she'd pointed to the cliff. Something about the cliff and not the cave. The deaths had nothing to do with the drugs even if Patrick had changed his mind about helping. She had a feeling the only person who knew the truth about why he backed out and his possible death was also dead.

They had to find the car with the missing taillight. She nudged Ryan. "We're wasting our time here," she whispered for his ears only.

"Why?"

She led him deeper into the trees and told him her suspicions.

"You believe this has to do with Mrs. Kim's illegitimate son and not drugs at all?"

"Yes. Grandmother didn't point to the cave. She pointed to the cliff. Brendan said he owns the cliff and Mrs. Kim wanted to buy it from him."

Ryan narrowed his eyes. "How could a cliff cause two homicides?"

"I don't know. But I think we need to find out." She motioned to Detective Kane. "Tell him I want to go back to Leilani's."

"You know I don't like lying to law enforcement." Ryan crossed his arms and stared at her.

"Then tell him I want to talk to Mrs. Kim and I think, other than catching drug smugglers, this is a waste of time for catching a murderer."

"He'll find the other more believable." Ryan sighed and walked back to where the detective was watching the ocean.

~*~

"You do know it's not a good idea to bring up a person's past when you don't know them very well,"

Ryan said as he parked the rental car in front of the Kim residence. Shandra had been quiet on their drive. Knowing her, she was busy putting all the pieces she'd collected together and figuring out what she was going to say.

Detective Kane had questioned him about Shandra wanting to give up on the stakeout when she'd been so gung-ho to solve the deaths. Ryan wanted to say because she was following her dreams and her gut, but very few in law enforcement understood his wife's skills.

Shandra stepped out of the car as his phone buzzed. It was Jenny.

"Hold on," he called out and took the call. "Hey, what's up?"

"I know who has the vehicle with one taillight."

This was good to know. "Who?"

"Saul Southwell."

He couldn't stop the smile spreading on his face. He'd known the guy was no good. "Did you tell Detective Kane? He'll need that info for his drug bust."

"And the murder."

Ryan shot a glance at the front door. Where had Shandra gone? "I have to go." He disconnected the call and sprang out of the car.

He hadn't noticed the front door open. She must have wandered around to the back. Where Elijah lived. He wasn't sure how much the young artist was mixed up in all of this considering his girlfriend had been killed.

He ran around the house in time to see Elijah let Shandra into his bungalow. His heart raced as he ran across the lawn to the pool area.

"Where are you going?" a woman's voice called out to him.

He didn't respond or look back, he continued running toward the bungalow. That's when he realized the beating of his heart was keeping time with the blaring rock beat filling the air. How could they talk with that racket? It would be perfect to hide a scream.

Ryan knocked the door open with his shoulder and stopped.

Shandra and Elijah were looking at a painting. They both had tears in their eyes.

He walked across the room and turned the record player off before joining them.

The painting was of Billie, leaning over a pottery wheel. She had clay on her hands, arms, cheeks. She wore overalls, a bandana, and a smile that said she loved what she was doing and the person looking at her.

"This is beautiful," Shandra said. "Did you know much about her family?"

"No. She didn't like to talk about them. I don't even know who to call about arrangements. The police still have her body." He stared at the picture. "Who would want to hurt her?"

Shandra led him over to one of the two chairs in the studio area. "Sit. I'd like to ask you some questions."

Ryan poked around in the kitchenette area and found some cold drinks. He gave one to Elijah and the other to Shandra before finding a folding chair to sit on.

"What kind of questions?" Elijah was coming back to his broody self.

"Questions that could lead us to who killed Billie." Shandra felt Ryan sitting between her and the door. She was thankful he was allowing her to do the talking.

"You think I know who killed her?" Elijah had been melancholy when she'd arrived. Now, with the portrait to the side, he was becoming belligerent. A quality he didn't get from his father.

"You may know who did without realizing it." Shandra took a deep breath and started. "Why were you and she pretending to not be a couple anymore?"

"I was tired of living here with Mrs. Kim always putting her nose in my business. Saul told us of a way to make extra money. He said all Billie had to do was give Patrick the numbers he gave her, and we'd get a thousand for each time she delivered." Elijah wiped a hand over his face. "That's why she was killed, right? Because we wanted out of here."

"Why did she pretend to be mooning over Patrick?" Shandra didn't understand that part.

"Saul thought he might do something stupid like go to the cops. So, she hung around him to let Saul know if he did." Elijah frowned. "She was paid extra to do that." He waved a hand. "Ever since I agreed to live here, I've felt like I was in jail. Mrs. Kim said, she has a friend with an art gallery who is going to do a showing, and then I'll have lots of money. But so far, all she does is take the paintings and I haven't seen a dime. I have to go to her for money for groceries." He glanced around the bungalow. "I hate it here."

"Who do you think killed Patrick?" Shandra asked.

Elijah rubbed his hands together. "The same person who killed Billie." He peered into her eyes. "If I say, I'll be the next body found."

She changed the direction of her questions. "Where were you born?"

He frowned. "What does that have to do with anything?"

"Nothing. I was curious."

A rooster crowed.

"A small town in Michigan. My parents died in a car accident when I was sixteen. I headed for warm weather and sunny skies and ended up in Oahu. That's where Mrs. Kim found me. She brought me to Kaua'i."

"How long did you know Mrs. Kim before you moved here?" Shandra wondered if maybe she'd been off on this being the child of Mrs. Kim and Brendan Darnell.

"She was at an art exhibit in Oahu a couple years ago. She expressed interest in my work. Bought a couple of pieces and then I didn't see her again until she offered me the chance to stay in her bungalow for free and paint. She said she belonged to the Kaua'i Art Society and could make sure my paintings were in all the galleries and exhibitions on the island. Who wouldn't jump at an offer like that?" He made a face. "I didn't know about all the strings attached until I was happily painting away here."

"Did she like Billie?" Shandra had a feeling Billie might have been part of the reason the artist was trying so hard to get away from his benefactor.

"She didn't come out and say it, but I saw her watching from a window when Billie would be crossing the pool area. The expression on her face wasn't one of pleasure." His hands flexed into fists. "Did she kill Billie?"

Shandra ignored that and moved on. "Have you ever seen Mrs. Kim with Saul?"

He grinned. "Billie and I were skinny-dipping in

the pool one night when we heard someone drive up. I jumped out, saw it was Saul, and jumped back in, figuring they wouldn't come out to use the pool. Billie said she was hungry and was going to raid the old lady's fridge. That's what we called Mrs. Kim." He stopped smiling. "She was gone a while and came back without any food. She said she almost got caught and that was all she said. But she started acting weird around Saul after that."

"You think she did get caught and that's why she was different when Saul was around?" Shandra could see that would be awkward if the young woman had been caught eavesdropping.

"I don't think she was caught. Because Mrs. Kim didn't act any different toward Billie. I think she heard something and didn't know whether to tell me or not."

"Did Billie keep a diary?" Shandra asked.

"No. All she had was what she called an idea pad." He stood. "She left it here most of the time. She said I gave her more ideas than anyone or thing else." His eyes glistened as he walked over to the corner where he'd propped up the portrait of Billie. He picked up a small backpack and carried it back across the room. "This was her stuff."

"That's all she kept here?" Shandra said, surprised that she had so little given how much time she had spent here.

"We didn't want the old lady to know she was practically living here." He snorted. "I know she came in and looked around when I wasn't here. I could tell."

Chapter Thirty-one

Shandra carried the small pack to the rental car.

"What are you thinking?" Ryan asked. "You found out a lot, but did you find out if he is Mrs. Kim's son?"

"He's not." She sat in the car and started going through the pack. "I think Billie's house was looked through, not for the book they wanted from Patrick, but for the book that Elijah was talking about."

"Her idea book? Why?"

"I'm guessing she wrote down the conversation she overheard." Shandra found the hardbound sketch book in the back pocket of a pair of shorts at the bottom of the bag. She pulled it out and flipped through the pages. "She had some wonderful ideas for her next projects," she muttered. And there it was in capital letters. SAUL IS OLD LADY'S SON

She grinned. The young woman had sense enough to not name Mrs. Kim. However, after her conversation with Elijah, Shandra knew exactly who Billie meant.

Ryan pulled out his phone.

"Who are you calling?"

"Detective Kane. We know who killed both Patrick and Billie. I would say for two different reasons, but when Billie figured it out, she probably went to Saul to get Elijah loose of Mrs. Kim and instead he killed her. Jenny called when you got out of the car. The car with the one taillight belongs to Saul."

Shandra hoped they could find him before he hurt anyone else. "I think we need to get Elijah away from here. What if Mrs. Kim says we were talking to him to Saul?" She leaped back out of the car and ran to the back of the house.

She saw the backs of Saul and Elijah heading through the trees. There hadn't been any other vehicles in front of the house. Where had he come from? Not waiting for Ryan, she raced to where she'd last seen the two and realized it was a well-worn path. Would the two circle around to the front of the house where Ryan would see them?

Going slow to avoid making any noise, Shandra pulled out her phone and texted Ryan. *Saul has Elijah. On path in trees.*

Ryan replied, *Come back.*

At that moment she caught sight of the two. They'd left the path. Saul was shoving Elijah toward the cliff edge.

Hurry Saul is going to force him off the cliff.

There was only one thing to keep him from shoving the young artist off the cliff. Shandra ran out into the open.

"Saul, what are you doing here?" she called.

The man spun around. He had a gun in his hand.

Elijah sprinted away from him and ducked down over the edge of the cliff.

Saul realized he'd lost the painter and waved his gun at her. "What are you doing here?"

"Looking for Elijah. Why did you have a gun on him?"

He laughed. "For the same reason I have one on you. You both know too much."

"What do you think we know?" She had to keep him talking until Ryan caught up to them.

His eyes narrowed. "I know everyone you've been talking to."

"Okay. I know you killed Patrick and Billie."

He laughed. "There's no proof."

"How long have you been running around with only one taillight?"

He swore and waved his gun. "If you hadn't come here, that do-gooder Leilani would have had to go with the juror Mother picked and my whiny Father would have had to go into the laundering business."

"Drop your weapon!" Ryan shouted from somewhere to her left.

Saul's arm swung that direction in slow motion.

"No!" Shandra screamed as the boom of a gun rang out and the acrid scent of a fired weapon floated on the sea breeze.

~*~

Ryan disarmed Saul, who lay withering on the ground clutching his right shoulder. The sound of sirens rang through the air as he strode over to Shandra, swaying as if her legs were about to give out.

He wrapped his arms around her. "Where is Elijah?"

She pointed. "He dived over the cliff when I called out to Saul. Thank you for arriving when you did."

He kissed her and led her over to the edge of the cliff where she'd pointed. Elijah was sitting about ten feet down, his arms wrapped around himself, staring at the ocean.

"You can come up. It's safe," Ryan called down to the young man.

Elijah glanced up, saw the two of them, and scrambled to his feet. He crawled with his hands and feet up the side of the rocky cliff.

He hugged Shandra. "When I heard the gun, I thought I'd left you up there to die."

She gave him a one-armed hug. "I'm glad you ran when you did. He didn't have anyone to use for a shield when Ryan arrived."

Ryan was happy about that as well. He'd feared having to try and free the two of them.

"Saul! Saul! My baby!" Mrs. Kim ran across the area between the trees and the cliff ahead of three officers and Detective Kane. The woman dropped to her knees beside the man clutching his arm.

He must have figured they had him because he hadn't tried to get away while Ryan's back was turned.

"Come on. The police will need your statements," he said to Shandra and Elijah.

They joined the small group that now had Saul handcuffed. Mrs. Kim was crying, consoling Saul, and trying to intimidate the police all at the same time.

Ryan led Shandra over to a downed log at the edge of the trees. "Why didn't you come back when I told you?"

She peered into his eyes. "I didn't want another

young artist to lose his life when I could stop it. I called out to Saul. When he swung around, Elijah took off." She smiled. "I knew then that you would have an easier time of getting him."

"He could have killed you as soon as he saw me." Ryan put an arm around her shoulders. They'd been in situations like this before. She never listened. Her need to follow her grandmother's dreams and her need for justice always put her in harm. He just had to be there every time to make sure she survived.

~*~

Detective Kane, Ike, sat in Leilani's living room. He was without his badge and gun. Shandra smiled at how he and Leilani had grown closer since the murders of Patrick and Billie had been solved.

"I don't understand," Leilani said. "We both thought Elijah was the love child of Louise and Brendan. How did you change your mind? And why did Patrick and Billie have to die?"

Ike and Ryan stared at Shandra. She took that as consent to tell Leilani what she'd figured out. "I'll start with the murders. Patrick was killed because he didn't want to help smuggle in drugs any more. The painting was his way of showing what he knew and had a record of it. Kind of like, 'Hey, leave me alone or I'll tell everything.'" She glanced at her husband. He nodded. "After Patrick's display at the gallery, I think Saul was worried that he would give them up."

"But Patrick was alive when I showed up and Saul was leaving." Leilani picked up her glass of iced tea.

"I, we, believe, he parked somewhere and doubled back, having you as the last person to see him and after you tried to save Patrick, you made the perfect patsy.

Patrick had shouted at you at the event, you went out there, fought with him, and shoved him over the edge. Saul waited for you to leave, finished the job and walked back to his car."

"He was standing on the cliff when I arrived that night." Ryan added. "He and a few other people, but I thought it odd that he was there. He hadn't had good things to say about Patrick after he'd left."

"And poor Billie? I didn't have a clue she and Elijah were still together. He has to be heart-broken." Leilani put the drink down and clasped her hands in her lap.

Shandra could feel her friend's empathy for those dead and the living who had loved them. "Billie overheard a conversation between Saul and Mrs. Kim. She realized he was her son and that she knew about the drug dealing he was doing. I think she confronted Saul about the knowledge and used blackmail—she wouldn't tell anyone if he let them out of the drug smuggling. She might have mentioned she had it written down. That's why her place was ransacked. Her mistake was confronting Saul about that. He killed her and went on his run, talking to a woman so he had an alibi."

"Forensics had her death earlier than he said he went on his run," Ike said. "When I questioned that, he said she was sleeping in the hammock when he went on his run. How was he supposed to know she was dead already?"

"Okay, you covered the deaths, what about the parentage?" Leilani asked.

Shandra shrugged. "I could tell they were close in age, but I believed Mrs. Kim would keep her son close. I didn't dream he'd be the one running things."

"Saul has been here for ten years. Does that mean he and Louise knew they were mother and son that long?" Leilani asked this question to Ike.

"We've discovered that she never gave him up for adoption. She had a relative raise him with money she sent and she visited him on his birthday and whenever Mr. Kim would make a trip to San Francisco." Ike settled back into the couch. "I think she started up the drug smuggling before her husband died. And brought Saul over to help her with it."

Leilani shook her head. "Why would a mother use her child to do something illegal?"

"Who knows? It is something that psychologists are always trying to figure out," Ike said.

"So when did you know?" Leilani asked Shandra.

"For sure? When I saw Billie's book, it confirmed what I had started to figure out after talking with Elijah. He had no affection for the woman. And he wanted out of the arrangement they'd made. Again, most parents wouldn't steal from their child, which was basically what she was doing with Elijah. She took his paintings, told him she was giving them to a gallery for a showing, and then she pocketed the money and only doled out little bits to him to keep him at her mercy and painting."

"I'm glad to know that Brendan didn't want to launder money, that it was all Francie and her mom's deal." Leilani shifted to study Ike. "What happened to those two?"

"They will be coming up for assault and kidnapping for hitting you and tying you up." Ike frowned. "We can't connect them to the laundering because it hadn't happened yet. But we do have phone calls between Francie and Saul and witnesses to seeing her at his house the night we believe Billie showed up and was killed. And she is the one who called the reporter that was at the gallery the night we found the drugs."

"Who put the drugs there?" Leilani asked.

"From what we gathered from Francie, it was her mother. They sent those people in to look for the drugs and then call the police. But when Shandra confronted them, they ran out." Ike studied Shandra. "What is it about you that you always seemed a step ahead of me?"

Ryan's phone started beeping. "That's our cue to head to the airport. Leilani, thank you for your hospitality." He hugged her. And held his hand out to Ike. "And thank you for not putting me in jail for getting in the way."

The two men shook. Ike slapped Ryan on the shoulder. "*Mahalo*. Without you and your lovely wife, it would have taken us longer to get to the truth. Safe travels."

"*Mahalo*," Ryan said, heading to the door.

Shandra stood. She hugged Leilani. "Don't ask me back next year. I've had enough Hawaiian excitement for a while."

"I'm so sorry you were dragged into this." Leilani's voice cracked.

"I'm not. If we hadn't been here, you would have been sitting in jail all this time." Shandra faced Ike. "Thank you for understanding and allowing us to help."

"*Mahalo* to you and your husband. I wasn't sure what to think of you two, but you do make a good team." Instead of shaking her hand, he pulled her into a big bear hug. "I'm glad your husband arrived in time to keep you safe."

"Me too."

"Come on. You're the one who can't wait to get home," Ryan said from the front door.

"Bye."

"*Aloha*!" Leilani and Ike said in unison.

Shandra walked out to the rental car, drew in one more sweet breath of plumeria and moist heat, and looked forward to inhaling the pine-scented, crisp air of Huckleberry Mountain and hearing Sheba's barks of delight, Lil's grumbles mixed with happiness, and her horses' whinnies. While it was always an experience to travel, she welcomed the comfort of home.

~*~

About the Author

Thank you for reading ***Abstract Casualty.*** The research for this book started when I finally talked my husband into going to Hawaii with me. Between hiking to remote beaches and discovering the island, I learned about the art community on Kaua'i. It had the perfect event to which I could bring Shandra and that started the process of how I plotted ***Abstract Casualty***.

I hope you will continue to follow Shandra and Ryan's investigations. I will continue to write their stories as long as I can come up with believable, interesting murders.

If you enjoyed this book, please leave a review. It is the best way to thank an author for an enjoyable read. I love to hear from fans.

All my work has Western or Native American elements in them along with hints of humor and engaging characters. My husband and I raise alfalfa hay in rural eastern Oregon. Riding horses and battling rattlesnakes, I not only write the western lifestyle, I live it.

You can contact or follow me at these places:

Website: http://www.patyjager.net
Blog: https://writingintothesunset.net/
FB Page: https://www.facebook.com/PatyJagerAuthor/
Amazon: https://www.amazon.com/Paty-Jager/e/B002I7M0VK
Pinterest: https://www.pinterest.com/patyjag/
Twitter: https://twitter.com/patyjag
Goodreads:
http://www.goodreads.com/author/show/1005334.Paty_Jager